S0-AQC-884

The
GRAVEYARD

Written by

ROSALYN RIKEL RAMAGE

Rosalyn R. Ramage

Order this book online at www.trafford.com
or email orders@trafford.com

Most Trafford titles are also available at major online book retailers.

© Copyright 2012 Rosalyn Rikel Ramage.
All rights reserved. No part of this publication may be reproduced, stored in a retrieval
system, or transmitted, in any form or by any means, electronic, mechanical, photocopying,
recording, or otherwise, without the written prior permission of the author.

Printed in the United States of America.

ISBN: 978-1-4669-5033-7 (sc)
ISBN: 978-1-4669-5034-4 (e)

Library of Congress Control Number: 2012913790

Trafford rev. 08/10/2012

 www.trafford.com

North America & international
toll-free: 1 888 232 4444 (USA & Canada)
phone: 250 383 6864 ♦ fax: 812 355 4082

For my grandsons,
Willis, Zach, and Foster

****

Special thanks are extended to many people who have read and made contributions to the development of this book, especially to my children—Rae Ellyn Kelley, Ron Ramage, and Risa Robinson—who have assisted and encouraged me in many ways—and to my sister, Maralyn Rikel, who has provided personal support as well as historical information. Specific acknowledgment is given to students at Barfield Elementary School, Eakin Elementary School, and DuPont Hadley Middle School as they encouraged me to share my story. But without the continued dedicated support and encouragement of my husband, Donald Ray Ramage, this book would never have become a reality.

The portrait on the following page depicts some of my own ancestors. You will find that Emma Mae, the tall 12-year old girl on the back row, is the storyteller in the book. Edward, her 10-year old brother, is in the middle of the picture (second row), and 7-year old Fred (sitting on his father's knee), is also a major character.

All of my books include fact, fiction, fantasy, and family values.

THE FAMILY (Photograph Circa 1914)
Front row: Frederick, William, Arthur
Middle Row: Papa, Edward, Mama
Back Row: Emma Mae and Clarence

MINI-GLOSSARY OF GERMAN WORDS AND PHRASES USED IN THE STORY:

Auf Wiedersehen	Goodbye
Bereit, fertig, los!	Ready, set, go!
Danke	Thank you
Einundachtzig	Eighty-one
Ein, zwei, drei, LOS!	One, two three, GO!
Fraulein	Young lady
Gesundheit!	Good health, but sometimes used as the expression for (God) bless you, especially following a sneeze!
Gute Nacht	Good night
Guten Morgen	Good morning
Guten Tag	Good day
Ja	Yes
Junger Mann	Young man
Kapitan	Captain
Kinderlein	Little children
Mutter	Mother
Nein	No
Piraten!	Pirates!
Schon, wirklich schon	Beautiful, really beautiful
So sei es!	So be it!

GERMAN SENTENCES IN TEXT:

Das ist gute.	This is good.
Geh weg!	Go away!
HALT! Das ist nicht gut	STOP! This is not good!
Ich heisse Emma Mae.	My name is Emma Mae.
Sei guten Mutes.	Be of good cheer.
Sie haben einen anderen Blinden passagier?	You found another stowaway?
Wir fanden einen anderen Blinden passagier?	We found another stowaway!

CHAPTER 1

"Hold on, Emma Mae! He's runnin' for home!" Edward hollered near my ear. I was clinging wildly to the mane of our big horse as he galloped down the hillside at top speed. Since we were riding bareback, there was no saddle horn to hold onto. I stretched forward as far as I could reach and finally grabbed the reins that were flapping wildly in the wind. Billy Buck continued racing down the rut-filled dirt lane toward the gravel road below.

Finally, I got enough control to draw back hard on the reins. "Whoa, Billy Buck," I called, pulling on the leather straps. "Whoa, boy. Slow down." Now that I had the reins, the horse began to respond to my tugs and slowed his pace. "Good horse! Good boy!" I called in my most convincing twelve-year old voice.

My ten-year old brother Edward was still clinching me tightly around the waist. He joined me in saying soothing words to the frightened horse as it gradually slowed to a walking pace.

"Whoa now," I said once again. The horse finally stopped at the place where the long downhill lane from my aunt's house came out onto the gravel road. "Let's get off, Ed, and let him settle down."

Edward quickly slid off the horse, then reached to help me down. Both of us went to Billy Buck's head and stroked the horse's neck and face.

"What got into him, Edward? He never bolted like that before with us on his back."

"There must have been a noise that scared him. Or maybe he saw a snake in the grass. He tried to run from Papa in the field one day when he saw a snake crawlin' across his path."

"He seems okay now," I commented, "but let's lead him along the road for a while so he can settle down some more."

We set out in the direction of home that was located only a short distance away. Soon we found ourselves walking along the vine-covered fence at the edge of a large, meadow-like area known as the Singleton Field. This land belonged to a wealthy man who lived in town. None of us knew much about Mr. Singleton except that he owned this property that was named for him.

Many years ago, we had been told, our great-grandfather had made arrangements to have a family burial spot that would be located at the far end of the field, away from the railroad tracks. Since then, all of our ancestors had been buried here. Trees and bushes were scattered among the old tombstones.

"Do you get the heebie-jeebies when you walk past the graveyard?" I asked.

"Not really," Edward responded. "It's just the graves of people in our family who used to live in this area before they died."

"You're right. I wish I knew some of the stories about them, though, especially of our older ancestors."

"It would be interesting to know some of the old stories, for sure" he said, "but today I'm wonderin' about the story that goes with the hat hangin' here on this fencepost."

"This straw hat?" I asked pointing to a battered-looking hat perched on top of a post.

"Yeah, I see it hangin' here every once in awhile, but I never see anybody around that it might belong to. There's a little trail, though, that leads from the hat on the post through the graveyard to the woods over yonder."

I stopped Billy Buck so we could look across the cemetery. The late afternoon sun filtered through the leaves. Birds chattered in the trees while bees buzzed and butterflies fluttered in the wild flowers.

Suddenly I had an urge to go inside the graveyard to see my great-grandmother's grave. Mary Katherine and her husband Johann had brought their family from Germany to this part of the world many years ago. She had died long before I was born, but I had heard stories about what a wonderful storyteller she had been. She had been known as the Queen of Storytelling. At least, that's what Mama had told me.

"Edward," I said. "Let's tie Billy Buck to this post so we can walk in the cemetery for a minute. I'd like to check out the dates when Great-Grandmother lived."

Edward glanced up at the sun that was hanging low in the sky. "If we do, we can't stay long. We've got to get back to the house in time to do our chores."

"I know. I only want to stop for a minute or two."

"It's all right with me," he said. "Besides, I've been wantin' to go to the edge of the woods to see if I can tell who's been goin' in and out over there. The person this hat belongs to might have some funny business goin' on inside the woods."

I tethered the horse to the post. He immediately began munching the roadside grass. Edward held the top barbed wire up with his hand and pushed the bottom one down with his foot, making a large opening for me to crawl through. Then I did the same for him.

As we walked into the cemetery, golden beams of sunlight slanted across the tombstones, causing them to glow eerily. Since nobody paid much attention to keeping the graveyard cleared, there were weeds and wildflowers growing all around.

Right away I spotted the graves of our grandparents, John and Annie Kate. They were close to the front of the cemetery.

I had to search a bit, though, before I located the monument of our great-grandparents. Pushing the weeds aside, I knelt down in front of it and read the words that were engraved on the large stone. On the left side of the stone, I saw the name of my great-grandfather Johann, but the words I was really looking for were on the right side. It had the words engraved: "Mary Katherine, Queen of Storytelling, 1805-1870."

I sat down and leaned back against the stone. A small creek trickled nearby on its way to the larger stream at the edge of the field. It was all very peaceful.

I noticed that Edward was taking care to stay on the trail as he crossed the graveyard toward the woods. We had jokingly been told that it could bring bad luck or rile up the spirits of the dead if you stepped on a grave.

In that quiet moment, my thoughts returned to my ancestor named Mary Katherine. It made me feel proud to know that she was actually buried here in this spot, so near our home. What would it have been like, I wondered, to leave your homeland and cross the ocean to a new place and a new way of life like she and her family had done? As I sat relaxing, thinking about this, I nonchalantly pulled on the tiny gold chain with a cross on it that was around my neck. I had a habit of doing that.

Suddenly Edward came running back across the graveyard path. "Come on, Sis! Let's get out of here." He grabbed my hand. "Hurry! We've got to go. Now!"

He pulled me up and we dashed toward the fence. Once again he held it open for me to crawl through. When we were both on the other side, he untied Billy Buck's reins. He made his hands into a loop for me to step in as I climbed back up onto the horse's back. Then I hauled him up so he could straddle the horse behind me.

"Let's go," Edward said. I made a clicking sound with my mouth to urge the horse to walk quickly down the road toward home.

"All right, Edward. Now you can tell me why we're in such a hurry. Why are you so scared?"

"I still don't know what's goin' on back there in the woods," he answered, "but it looks like people are havin' a meetin' in there. They were carryin' on and makin' noise. I only got a peek at them through the bushes, but, from what I saw, it was definitely not supposed to be happenin' in these woods. Can you get Billy Buck to move any faster?"

I used my knees to push against the horse's sides. He immediately responded by picking up speed. He trotted over the railroad tracks near our home. I asked, "Do you think they are up to mischief, Ed?"

"There's no way I can know about that, but I *do* know it looked like something was goin' on that shouldn't be."

"Are you going to tell Papa about it?" I asked my brother as the horse slowed down and turned into our own lane that led to the barn behind the house.

Edward paused. Then he said, "*Nein.* I don't want to get involved—at least not yet. We'll just watch for a while and see if we notice anything else."

I found out later that Edward had seen three things when he peeked around the sassafras bushes that he didn't tell me. First, one of the boys in the secret party in the woods had spotted him spying on them. Second, Edward knew that boy. It was none other than Clyde—the bully and terror of Sunny Slope School! And, third, Ed was pretty sure the thing Clyde had pointed in his direction was a shotgun!

CHAPTER 2

When we got to the barn, we put the horse inside and hurriedly climbed over the fence that separated the barn lot from the backyard. We ran up the steps onto the back porch and opened the screen door. Mama was standing there waiting for us with the baby on her hip and a scowl on her face.

"There you are," she said crossly. "It sure took you long enough to take that basket of purple hull peas to Aunt Emma's house. Since I let you ride the horse, I thought you'd be back in no time, but here you are, getting home when the sun's almost set."

"We're sorry, Mama, but Billy Buck got spooked by something and ran down Aunt Emma's hill. We almost fell off, he was running so fast," I explained.

Edward joined in. "That's right, Mama, so after we got him calmed down we decided to walk along with him. It took a little longer, but he seemed to like it that way."

I noticed that he left out the part about the cemetery, so I didn't mention it, either.

"Well," Mama said. "You have your chores to do, and I've got to get busy finishing up supper." She looked at me. "Emma Mae, you take care of the young 'uns." She handed Baby Arthur to me. He smiled and clapped his hands. "Take him out in the backyard while you take the clothes down off the clothesline. William and Fred are already out playing with the dog."

"All right, Mama," I said. "We're sorry we're late, but we'll pitch in now." I hugged the baby close as I carried him out the back door. I loved taking care of him, so I didn't consider it a chore.

I could hear Mama still fussing at Edward inside the kitchen. "You need to hurry on out to the barn and take care of the animals."

"Don't worry, Mama. I'll get it all done," I heard him say as he carried the slop bucket out the kitchen door. The screen door slammed shut behind him. As he walked across to the barn lot, some of the water from the bucket splashed out on the ground. This combination of table scraps and dishwater would be added to some dry food for the pigs' supper.

Baby Arthur sat in the grass to watch me while I took the clothes off the line. As I folded the stiff dry clothes and piled them in the basket, I played peek-a-boo with him. He laughed and patted his chubby little hands together.

Nearby, seven-year old Frederick and four-year old William were playing a game with Jiggs, our three-legged terrier. Jiggs had lost a back leg in a train accident when he was a puppy, but he had never let that slow him down. As a matter of fact, Jiggs had a very special talent. When he was in the right mood, he could hop around on his one hind leg. He especially liked to do this when music was being played.

Right now, though, he was playing a game of "Fetch" with the boys. They would throw a stick across the yard so Jiggs could run and catch it in midair, then bring it back to them.

When I finished folding the laundry, I plopped the clothesbasket on the back porch and picked the baby up. "Time to feed the chick-chicks," I said to Arthur I held him on my hip while I shelled the dry kernels off the corncobs for the chickens to eat. Then the baby and I gathered the eggs and carefully put them in the egg basket.

Our stopover by the cemetery flashed through my mind occasionally, but by now it seemed far away.

Edward brought the cows in from the pasture and took them to the milking stalls where he had their food waiting. I noticed Ed was careful to stay clear of Bossy, the lead cow, who sometimes liked to butt him with her horns.

By the time he finished his other routine jobs of putting out feed for the horses and slopping the hogs in the pigpen, Mama was calling us for supper. We all raced to see who could get to the back door first. Baby Arthur and I won! We trooped into the kitchen, washed up for supper, and sat down at the big kitchen table.

When Mama put the food on the table, who should show up but Papa and our fourteen-year old brother Clarence. It seemed like Papa always knew exactly how to plan it so they could get to the house in time to eat.

"Mmm-mmm, Mama," Papa said. "You shore got it smellin' good in here."

Suppertime was normal. We ate slab bacon, purple hull peas, and baked sweet potatoes. Tonight we had a treat. We stirred creamy butter into fresh sorghum molasses to go with our homemade bread.

After we finished eating and the kitchen was cleaned up, the entire family sat on the front porch for a while before bedtime, as we did almost every night. A coal oil lantern gave off a soft glow. Papa sat in his big wooden chair, smoking his pipe. The embers in the pipe glowed brightly in the near-darkness.

Mama was in the wooden rocker, holding Baby Arthur. Clarence sat on the steps, whittling something out of wood. The rest of us were squeezed in the porch swing. It made squeaky sounds as we swayed back and forth, back and forth. Heat lightning flashed in the distance while lightning bugs flickered nearby.

"Well, children," Mama said, "tomorrow's the first day of school for three of you."

"I know," I replied excitedly, "and I can hardly wait!"

"I'm anxious to meet the person we've heard about who might be our new teacher this year," Edward said. "We've never had a man teacher before."

"Yeah," seven-year old Fred chimed in. "*Any*body will be better than that bad old Miss Stone we had last year."

"Now, now, Freddie." It was Papa's turn to speak. "I know Miss Stone was strict and expected a lot out of you, but that don't mean she was bad."

Fred took up for himself. "I was just saying what I heard Clarence say."

Clarence jerked his head around. "Who? Me? Why, I'm not even going back to that dumb school this year. Why would I say a silly thing like that, Silly?"

"Young man," Mama said sharply. "Your Papa and I are keeping you home this year to help on the farm, but that's no reason for you to talk smart to your little brother."

"That's right, Clarence," Papa agreed. "We've decided to take you out of school 'cause we need your help around here on the farm, but you've still got lots of learnin' to do. And name callin' is *not* one of the things we'll abide by."

"Why can't you just hire somebody to help with the work, Papa, and let Clarence go back to school so he can finish eighth grade?" I asked. I usually didn't speak my mind like that, but I felt sorry for my big brother for having to drop out of school.

"That's the way they used to do it back in the old country, Emma Mae. It's a family tradition. As the sons get older, they have to pitch in and help out."

"By 'the old country,' Papa, you mean Germany?" Edward asked.

"*Ja.* Our ancestors were farmers and fruit growers in the hill country of Germany before they came to this country to start a new life. They left everything behind. We owe them a lot, and keepin' traditions is one way we can show our respect."

"We understand that, Papa, but keeping Clarence at home just doesn't seem fair to Ed and me." I continued to argue the case for my older brother.

"I'm much obliged to you young'uns for takin' up for your brother, but Mama and I have made our decision, and that's that."

I didn't tell Papa, but he sounded a lot like last year's schoolteacher, Miss Olma Gayle Stone. Miss Stone often used the expression "and that's that" to mark the end of a discussion.

By this time Baby Arthur was asleep in Mama's lap. William, who had climbed in my lap earlier, was asleep, too. Fred, sitting between Edward and me in the swing, yawned. I knew it was time for us to go inside, but I had one more thing to say.

"Papa, before we go to bed I've got something I want to ask."

"What's that, Emma Mae?"

"I'm just wondering, do you think your ancestors ever regretted leaving Germany to bring their family to America?"

He puffed on his pipe for a minute before he answered. The coals glowed red in the darkness as the pungent smoke filled the air. "That's a good question, little *Fraulein*. And the answer to your question, young lady, is '*nein*'. No, I heard my grandparents say, many a time, that when they changed their country, they changed their hearts. No, ma'am, I think yonder cemetery is filled with people who felt they made the right decision for their families. May their souls rest in peace."

For some reason, those words gave me a strange tingle.

It was time to go inside to bed. All of us except Papa and Clarence stood to say good night.

"Clarence," I heard Papa say as the screen door closed softly behind me, "I reckon you'd best hitch up the wagon, come mornin', and take the young'uns to school on their first day back."

"Do I have to?" whined Clarence.

"*Ja*. We can spare you the time," Papa replied. "And that's that."

As I carried my little brother to bed, I noticed the portrait of my great-grandparents that hung on the wall in the parlor near the front door. They were wearing small smiles as they stared straight ahead at some unknown object. But, I wondered, were those small smiles turning up the corners of their lips . . . or sneers? Or were they simply puzzled? Or worried? Or maybe even angry? It was hard to tell, just looking at them. What might they have been thinking when the camera snapped their image so many years ago?

Papa's words came flashing back in my mind. "May their souls rest in peace," he had said. What does that phrase mean? I wondered as I tucked William in his bed. Without thinking, I whispered, "Rest in peace, little one." But as the words came out my mouth, a chill raced down my spine.

CHAPTER 3

Mama came to my bedroom to give me and my China doll, Maizey, a good night hug. As she left my room, I reached to grasp the gold necklace with the cross on it that she and Papa had given me for my twelfth birthday. I was very proud of it and had worn it around my neck ever since they gave it to me. But when I felt for the tiny chain, it wasn't there.

I jumped up and looked at my reflection in the mirror, hoping to see the chain in its usual place. I saw my dark, disheveled hair and my brown eyes looking back at me, but there was no necklace. It wasn't down the front of my nightgown, either, or in my bed. Where could it be? I wondered. Where *could* it be?

Suddenly, there was a flash in my mind. I recalled sitting by my great-grandparents' tombstone in the graveyard, winding the gold chain around my finger. Why, it must have come unfastened and fallen off by their monument.

Just as that image filled my mind, I heard a rumble of thunder in the distance. Oh, no, I thought. If it rains, the chain might wash away in that little creek and I might never be able to find it again. I couldn't stand the thought of losing it, so I reacted. I would go the cemetery now, before the rain began—but, even though it wasn't far away, I wouldn't dare go alone. Edward would have to go with me.

I hurriedly put my dress back on and tiptoed into the room that four of my brothers shared. I could hear sounds of snoozing all around as I crept to Edward's bed and gently shook him. He jumped straight up with a wild look in his eyes.

"Emma Mae," he whispered. "What are you doin' here?"

I put my finger to my lips and gestured for him to come with me. There was another sound of faraway thunder. Edward quietly got out of bed and pulled on his trousers before following me through the doorway.

"Ed," I whispered when we got to the kitchen that was located next to the bedrooms. "I know this will sound crazy, but I want you to go with me to the cemetery. Now. Tonight."

"What?" he responded in disbelief. "Why? Why tonight? What's so important that it can't wait until tomorrow?"

"I know it sounds crazy, but I'm pretty sure my special necklace fell off my neck while I was sitting by that big tombstone this afternoon. And there's a storm coming. I'm afraid it will be washed away down that little creek and will be gone forever." Another grumble of thunder sounded, a little closer this time.

Edward scratched above his left ear the way he always does when he's not sure about something. "I don't think we should go there, Emma Mae. Not tonight, especially with a storm comin'."

Tears sprang to my eyes. "But what if it's washed away? This could be my only chance to get it. I just can't bear to think about losing it."

"I really don't think we should," he said, "but if it's that important to you, let's go!"

He moved to the back screen door and quietly opened it. We both went out, being careful not to let it slam. The breeze that had been gentle earlier in the evening was picking up now. Dark clouds raced across the sky. The lightning flashes were still quite a distance away, but we knew we had to hurry if we wanted to get to the cemetery and back before the storm hit.

Hand-in-hand we walked on the dusty path that led around the house and out to the gravel road that ran in front of it. We broke into a fast trot as we ran up the little rise and across the railroad tracks. A little further along we came to the area where the cemetery was located.

"At least there's not a hat on the fencepost tonight," Edward noted as a lightning flash lit up the sky. The sound of thunder was growing closer. We climbed through the fence wires and hurried across the field to the cemetery.

"Why do I have such a creepy feeling that something strange is about to happen?" I whispered.

"I feel it, too," he muttered. "Probably because we're in a graveyard in the middle of the night."

I stopped and looked around with my hands on my hips. "What were we thinking, Ed? We came here without bringing a lantern or anything to help us see the chain if it's anywhere around." I was on the verge of tears.

"Beats me, Sis. I was still too sleepy to think, I guess. But since we're here, you need to show me the monument where you think you lost your necklace. Maybe we can see it shinin' when the lightnin' flashes."

I quickly led him to our great-grandparents' grave. The flashes were almost constant now. We got down on our hands and knees, searching for my necklace.

We hadn't been looking long when a zig-zag of lightning flared nearby. I thought I saw a glint of gold reflecting on the edge of the creek bank. Could it be? When another flash lit the scene as bright as day, I looked again. Yes! It was my gold chain!

"Here it is, Edward!" I shouted.

I reached and grabbed it just as there was another flare, but this time it didn't just flash and stop. Instead, lightning bolts began bouncing around the cemetery—exploding in the night around us like fireworks on the Fourth of July.

Then, as if the flashing lights were not enough, weird noises began to rise out of the ground around us. Ooooooo. Mournful and wailing sounds, they were, along with snickers and laughter. Ooooooooo. I had never heard anything so strange in all my life!

Shivers were running up and down my spine like a coon dog chasing a rabbit. The hairs on my arms stood straight out.

Now the sounds became more focused. Quavery voices asked questions like . . . "Who are you?" . . . "What are you doing here?" . . . "What do you want from us?" . . . "How can we help you?" The questions overlapped each other in a mysterious way.

Lightning bolts skipped from tombstone to tombstone as the trembling voices said strange words I didn't recognize . . . until I heard the word "*danke.*" Then I knew this language had to be German.

Edward and I stared at each other with big eyes and open mouths. Now other noises seemed to be rising from the ground. There was a sound like splashing water along with the hum of music and laughter and garbled voices.

A brilliant bolt of lightning was immediately followed by a clap of thunder that was so loud it shook the very ground where we were standing. Neither of us moved a muscle. Our eyes were as big as saucers as we stood there. We were as still as the tombstones in the graveyard around us.

Then—suddenly—nothing. The strange lightning quit flashing. The eerie sounds stopped abruptly. I continued to squeeze Edward's hand with one hand while clasping my necklace with the other. "Let's get out of here!" I cried.

"I'm with you, Emma Mae!"

We dashed to the fence and scrambled through the wires, but just as we started running toward home, from somewhere behind us came a low, mournful voice: "Fi-i-i-ind me!" We froze in our tracks. The voice called out again saying, "Fi-i-i-ind me!"

Edward and I stared at each other in the darkness. Without saying another word, we took off running like the wind, our bare feet skimming along the gravel road that ran along the edge of the Singleton Field, away from the graveyard, across the railroad tracks . . . to the safety of home.

Just as we ran onto the back porch, the rain began to fall. We watched through the screen door from the safety of the kitchen as the storm hit with all its fury.

I put my necklace around my neck and fastened the clasp before I looked at my brother. "Do you think we should tell Papa and Mama about what we saw and heard?" I asked him in a quiet voice.

He thought for a minute before replying, "No, I don't think so. They probably wouldn't believe us, anyway. They'd think it was just our imaginations." He continued looking out at the raging storm. "Besides, how could we explain goin' to the graveyard in the middle of the night?"

I reached out and hugged my brother. "Thanks, Ed, for going with me. You're the best."

"I'm just glad you found your special necklace," he said.

We both turned and headed to our rooms to go to bed, but in spite of everything, as I climbed into my bed, I couldn't get the words out of my head—"Fi-i-i-nd me! Fi-i-i-ind me!"

CHAPTER 4

The next thing I knew, Mama was calling me from the kitchen. "Emma Mae, it's time to get up for breakfast. You don't want to be late for school on the first day back."

I jumped out of bed and dashed to the kitchen door. Everything looked normal. What was I expecting? Ghosts from the graveyard? I ran to the window and looked out to see the freshly washed, sun-kissed world.

I ran across the room and planted a kiss on Mama's cheek. "*Guten Morgen, Mutter*! I'm so glad to see you on such a beautiful morning," I said, giving her a hug.

Mama smiled at this unexpected show of affection. "I'm glad to see you, too, my little *Fraulein*," she said, returning the hug.

"Why, *Mutter*, just look at that. Not only have you fixed breakfast, but you've already made our lunches." Mama nodded and smiled as she put a baked sweet potato, a chunk of homemade bread, and a big juicy pickle in each of the three shiny molasses buckets that were lined up on the table.

I quickly ate my fried egg and biscuit. With my mouth still full, I asked, "Where are the boys?"

"They were up early and had their breakfast a long time ago." Mama said.

"Sounds like I'd better hurry, then." I dashed to my room to get ready for school. The new dress Mama had made for me was hanging on a nail outside my closet. She had also made a big hair bow that matched. I put the dress on and pulled my hair back, attaching the bow behind my head. I liked what I saw in the mirror, especially the gold chain around my neck.

When I heard the whistle of the freight train as it rumbled past, I knew it was time to go. I picked my doll up and gave her a peck on the cheek. "Have a nice day here at home today, Maizey," I said. "I'm going back to school. Sorry you can't tag along this time." I plopped her down on the bed beside Maggie, my black cat. "You can't go either, Maggie, but I'll see you both this afternoon." I picked up my new tablet and grabbed my lunch pail off the kitchen table as I hurried through the house.

"Come on, boys. Let's go," I called as I walked out the front door. I didn't know that my brothers were already sitting in the front porch swing, waiting for me.

"We're ready when you are," Edward said.

I looked around to see both of them, holding new tablets and shiny lunch buckets. As was the custom on the first day of school, they were wearing their Sunday clothes. They were also wearing broad grins.

Jiggs sat between them in the swing. He looked like he was smiling, too. Since he thought he was a member of the family, he often barked like he was carrying on a conversation. Sometimes he seemed to be giving orders, as though he were the captain on a ship, we said.

"So what are we waiting for? Let's go!"

We hurried down the muddy path to the spring wagon with the team of horses hitched to it. They patiently swished their tails to keep the flies away. Clarence leaned against a wagon wheel with one leg crossed in front of the other, whittling on a stick with his pocketknife.

Mama carried Baby Arthur on her hip and held Little Will's hand as they walked across the yard. Papa came over to the wagon and boosted me up to my seat. Edward and Frederick scrambled up behind.

The family stood in a little group, waving good-bye. Jiggs barked and hopped around on his one hind leg.

"Mind your manners, children," Mama called. "Have a *guten Tag!*"

"You have a good day, too, *Mutter*," I called back.

"Hope your nice, good-looking new teacher we've been hearin' about is there, takin' the place of that Miss Stone," Papa said, smiling. "Have a good day. *Auf Wiedersehen!*"

"*Auf Wiedersehen!*" we hollered, waving at them. "Good-bye, Jiggs!"

Clarence clucked with his tongue so the horses knew it was time to go, but just as they started to move, there was a shout from behind. It was the four children who lived across the creek and down the lane from our house. They were hoping to catch a ride for the two-mile trip to school, and they had made it just in time!

As soon as they settled themselves in the back, Clarence said, "Giddy-up, Maud. Giddy-up, Billy Buck." The team of horses began to pull the wagon, slowly at first, then gradually picking up speed.

"Sunny Slope School, here we come!" Edward and I said at exactly the same time. We laughed at the timing of our remark, linking our little fingers together as we each made a wish. This was a little game of ours that we did, just for fun.

A wagon ride on a gravel road filled with ruts was a rough one, to say the least. Right away we jounced around as we started up the little hill beside our house. We were jostled even more as we went across the railroad tracks.

In almost no time we approached the Singleton Field where the cemetery was located. Edward and I, sitting on the middle bench seat of the wagon, could see over the top of the vine-covered fence. In the distance the gravestones looked dull and gray, in spite of the early morning sun that slanted down on them.

But wait a minute! Was it my imagination or were the stones actually beginning to glow as we approached?

"Look, Ed," I whispered in his ear, pointing toward the tombstones. "Do you see the light?" Bright, pulsating light had begun to flash once again, reminding me of lightning flashes. Small, fire-like balls bounced from gravestone to gravestone. The entire graveyard appeared to be glowing again . . . and it was definitely not from the sunlight. Goose bumps prickled my skin.

"How could I not see it when it's flashin' like that?" he murmured back. "It's too strange." But the strangest thing about it was that nobody else seemed to notice the flashing lights. As the wagon rolled on past the cemetery and up the road, we looked back. The gravestones, once again, were dull and gray. Edward and I stared at each other in bewilderment, shaking our heads, and shrugging our shoulders.

The next part of our ride on the narrow gravel road seemed to go quickly as we traveled around the curves and through the hills. The horses slowed as they pulled the wagonload of children up steep Babb's Hill, named for the Babb family who lived at the top. Once we got past their house, it wasn't long until Clarence pulled on the horses' reins to stop them. Then he guided them onto the larger hardened roadway that would take us to Sunny Slope School.

It seemed like no time before we saw the pointed belfry of the schoolhouse peeping over the next hilltop. As Clarence guided the horses into the wide gravel drive that led up the hill, we heard the school bell begin to clang. We knew it would be five minutes before we would be tardy.

Children of all ages and sizes were scattered around the schoolyard. Three girls stood by the well at the front of the school.

One of them was my cousin Pearl. She was also my best friend. They waved when they saw our wagon coming up the hill.

Not far from them stood Clyde, the Sunny Slope bully, and his younger brother Toby. Clyde was the biggest student in school—and the meanest! That's why all the children called him "Big Bad Clyde" behind his back.

Edward gasped. "Oh, no," he said, as a look of alarm spread across his face. "You might know old Clyde would be back at school."

"Why wouldn't he be back?" I asked. I didn't understand Edward's reaction to seeing the brothers.

"Oh, nothin'," he said. "I was just hopin' their parents had a tradition, too, that would keep Clyde at home this year so the rest of us wouldn't have to put up with him."

I nodded in agreement although I thought these remarks didn't sound like Ed's usual good nature. It seemed odd that he scrambled across me so he could get out of the wagon on the opposite side, away from Clyde, but I didn't ask why.

My friends came over to greet me and help me climb down from the wagon. As we moved away, I heard Clarence mumble, "I'm just glad it's you and not me coming back to this crummy school. I'd rather be doing anything than sitting there in that one room all day, looking at books."

I ignored him. Our little group was walking toward the door when another voice spoke behind us. I turned to look.

"Hey, Clarence, what'd you do? Bring all the little runts to school?" It was Clyde, standing by the horses, speaking in his loud, rude voice. Clyde was tall and thin. He had a sharp chin that jutted out. There were bumps all over his face.

Clarence just shook his head in response to Clyde's question.

We tried to ignore him, but he moved to stand in front of us as we walked toward the door, blocking our way. He grinned his smirky-looking grin. Up close like this, I could actually smell his breath. He always had bad breath. We stood there glaring at each other for several seconds.

The bell began to clang again, meaning it was time to take up books. Any latecomers who came after this would be in trouble. Clyde went on inside with Toby following him.

As my friends and I started into the building, I remembered my manners. "I'll be right there," I said to Pearl. "Save me a seat. I need to thank Clarence for the ride to school."

I turned back so I could wave my thanks, but I stopped short when I saw his face. He was still standing by the wagon, watching as we went into the schoolhouse, but he looked like he was on the verge of tears.

Our eyes met for an instant. Without saying a word, I smiled faintly, blew him a kiss, and waved good-bye. He smiled back at me, a sad little smile, then climbed up onto the wagon seat. He clucked his tongue. "Giddy-up" he said to the horses. They began walking slowly around the circle drive leading away from the schoolhouse. Surprised by the realization that my older brother would prefer to be back in school, I watched the wagon as it started down the hill.

Suddenly it occurred to me. I needed to get in my seat before the tardy bell stopped ringing! I rushed into the building, anxious to see if the new teacher was as good looking as the early rumors had said he was. When I saw the person ringing the bell, I stopped in my tracks! For there, standing in the middle of the room pulling the long rope to the bell, was the teacher. And it was obviously not the handsome young man we had been led to believe it might be. It was none other than Miss Olma Gayle Stone!

My eyes found Edward's as we exchanged looks of disbelief. After all we had heard about the new teacher, what could have happened? Why did the grown-ups in charge of hiring teachers go back to such an unpopular person? How could they do this to us?

I got to my seat just as Miss Stone looped the rope neatly into place. She walked to her desk, turned around and leaned against it with her arms crossed.

Her stout body was stiff, almost rigid, held upright by the tightly fitting corset she wore around her middle. Her starched white blouse fit high around her neck. The black skirt was long—but not long enough to cover up the high-topped lace-up shoes. Her graying hair was pulled back from her face and was wound into a tight bun at the back of her head. She wore a lot of powder on her face with so much rouge on her cheeks that it reminded me of a clown I had seen at the circus. Even from across the room, I could smell her talcum powder.

What I remembered most about Miss Stone, though, were her eyes. Her small, unframed glasses, which were always smudged, rested way down on her nose. She held her head tilted forward so she could look over the top of the glasses when she was talking. And when she looked at you, not only did she look *at* you—she *saw* you! I will never forget that long moment and the way she looked at each child in the room, wearing that permanent scowl.

"Young ladies and gentlemen," she said in her very proper way of speaking. "School is back in session. Summer vacation is over, so prepare your selves to work." She paused, looked at each of us again, then continued.

"I'm sure you will cooperate to the best of your ability throughout this school year." As she said this, she reached behind her and picked up a bundle of hickory switches from her desk. "A switch" she had explained to us last year, "is a twig or small limb that has been broken off a tree. It can be used like a whip to discipline a child who does not follow the directions of the elders." She held the bundle in her hands for just a moment, still looking around the silent room, making certain we were all aware of the switches. Satisfied, she laid them aside.

Next, she picked up the large Bible that she read from every day. "You will stand for our morning scripture reading to begin our day," Quietly, obediently, we all stood.

"I'm reading today from Psalm 118, verse 24. "'This is the day which the Lord has made. I will rejoice and be glad in it.'"

Be glad in it? I thought. I doubted if this woman had been glad for anything in her life!

Somehow we got through the day. At morning and afternoon recesses, instead of playing games, we mostly stood around talking about the teacher. Even Clyde was subdued. He didn't start a single fight all day.

Our neighbors joined us again as we walked home after school. We took the usual one-mile shortcut this time, crossing through the fields and creeks before coming out in the Singleton Field. We were nearly home.

As we cut across the field, I glanced at the nearby graveyard. The tombstones seemed to be glaring at me with disapproving, annoyed eyes and frowning, turned-down mouths.

We ran across the railroad tracks, down the hill, and into the house, anxious to tell Mama the bad news about the teacher. But as I hurried past the portrait of my great-grandparents, I paused. Today their expressions looked more like scowls of disapproval than the sneers they wore last night.

At bedtime that night, after Mama tucked my doll and me in bed, I wondered about things—like why had the first day of school seemed so special? Why had the cemetery glowed this morning? Why had it glared this afternoon? And why had the portrait scowled today? Why did it seem so unusually dark and feel so spooky in my room tonight? As I drifted off into a restless sleep, I tugged on my gold chain, wondering. What *does* it all mean?

CHAPTER 5

It felt as though I had just closed my eyes when Mama woke me up on the second day of school. It didn't take long to remember, though, that the second day of school is never the same as the first.

For instance, on the second day, you suddenly remember all the things that are *not* good about school that you had somehow forgotten on the first day of school. And you get ready with less enthusiasm. And you walk slower.

The neighborhood friends came to join Edward, Fred, and me again as we started out on the mile-long cross-country trek to school. We automatically climbed through the barbed-wire fence and walked along the trail across the Singleton Field. We trudged along slowly since none of us were anxious to see our teacher.

About midway across the field, I stopped abruptly. "What was that?" I asked in a sharp whisper.

"What was what?" seven-year old Frederick asked. Since I was holding his hand, he stopped beside me. Edward stopped, too. Everybody else, except the three of us, kept on walking. Edward and I looked at each other with big eyes.

"Did you see it, too?" I whispered to my brother.

"Of course I did," he whispered back.

"What's got into you two, anyway?" Fred asked. The others in the group had slowed down, looking back at us with curiosity.

"Probably nothing," I said, moving forward again. "I thought I saw some bright flashes of light over yonder in the graveyard, but I guess it was just the sun shining in my eyes."

Edward, falling into step beside me, muttered softly as he said, "It looked more like fireworks than sunlight, except there was no sound."

"I think you just made that up about lights flashing," Fred mumbled. "I didn't see any fireworks." We ignored him as we walked faster to catch up with the others.

The rest of the walk to Sunny Slope was normal. As we walked into the schoolyard, who should we see hanging around the well again, but Big Bad Clyde with his sidekick brother Toby. They sauntered in our direction just as the warning bell began to ring. We had five minutes 'til books.

"Well, if it ain't Miss Emma Mae and her puny little brothers," he said, singling us out again. He always wore that same kind of sneer when he talked like that. We kept on walking, ignoring his remark.

"Have you been out snoopin' around in any *graveyards* lately?" he asked, looking at Edward. "Seems to me like folks need to mind their own business, especially little boys who wear knickers to school."

I could feel Edward tensing as he walked beside me.

"Don't let him get to you, Ed, "I said softly. "You know that's just what he wants to do, so ignore him."

"What's that you're saying, little girl? Speak up so old Clyde can hear you. What's the matter? Cat got your tongue?"

He fell in step beside us as we walked toward the schoolhouse. Fred was holding tightly to my hand and I was holding onto Edward's arm, hoping to keep him from flying off at Clyde.

"Why, Emma Mae," Clyde said, "I do believe you're avoiding me. And here I am tryin' to be nice to you and your knock-kneed brothers."

Edward was clenching his fists now.

"Hold on a little longer, Ed," I whispered. "We're almost there."

But Clyde didn't stop. "Now that I'm thinkin' about it, you're actin' just plain stuck up! Everybody knows you and your family are the most snooty-actin' family around."

We were at the door of the building now. I knew Edward was about ready to start punching Clyde, which is exactly what Clyde wanted—to get somebody in trouble before school ever started. I pushed Edward in the door.

"I just don't know if I'm gonna be able to take it," he muttered as he walked toward his seat. Then he stopped and added, "I know something bad must be goin' on over there in the woods beside the graveyard, and he knows I know. But I don't care about that. It's just that he's gettin' to me, "

"And that's exactly my point," I whispered back. "He's doing this on purpose because he knows it bothers you. It doesn't bother me, so please, please, don't try to be a hero. Do what I say and ignore him."

Miss Stone started ringing the eight o'clock tardy bell, so we hurried to our seats. The morning routine began. All forty of us in the room were quiet and attentive, especially since she showed us the hickory switches again as she was talking to the large group.

Later in the day, when it was time for our history lesson, Miss Stone gave us older students an assignment. We couldn't believe our ears!

"For the older students in the school," she said, "I have your assignment for a major project. In one week you are to bring a report to school showing something about how your ancestors came to live in this part of the world."

She paused and peered over the top of her glasses at the students seated in the back of the room. After looking at each student, she moved to the chalkboard and continued. "Your projects will have four requirements." Here she picked up a stick of chalk and began to list her points on the big slate board. "Your assignment must be:

      (1) original

      (2) interesting

      (3) well researched

      (4) neatly written."

She turned back around to face us, obviously ignoring the looks of shock on all our faces. "Copy this assignment down on your tablets. Also make a note that these reports are not to be done by your parents, although they need to show evidence that your parents have helped with the information." She paused again. "Do you have any questions?"

Her question was met by silence. After a short pause, a quiet voice from the back of the room said, "Yes, ma'am." It was Pearl, daring to speak. "When did you say this report is due?"

Miss Stone turned toward Pearl and glared for a moment. Then she actually smiled—the kind of smile that turned up the corners of her mouth, but never reached her eyes. "One week from today," she answered flatly. "And that's that!"

At second recess that afternoon, the only topic of discussion was the assignment. A large assignment like this might be expected near the end of school, but on the second day? And to be completed in one week? It was unheard of!

We girls walked over to sit in the grass under the big elm tree. As usual, when there was a group of girls together, you could expect Big Bad Clyde to be hanging around, too. He shuffled over to where we were sitting, wearing that smirky look on his face. For some reason, he continued to focus on insulting my family and me today.

"Too bad Emma Mae won't be able to do the project," he said. "Since she's not interestin', don't know how to be original, and cain't write neat, she's gonna miss the boat altogether."

Everybody tried to act like Clyde wasn't even there. We kept talking amongst ourselves, but he seemed not to notice. He broke off a piece of tall dried grass and stuck the end of it in his mouth. He leaned against the trunk of the tree with his hands in the pockets of his overalls.

"But I guess the hardest part for Emma Mae will be the research," he said, looking at me with that hateful look. "Her parents ain't smart enough to help her with the research."

Suddenly, from out of nowhere, Edward appeared. He was swinging his fists madly at Clyde, hitting him on his chest and upper arms. Clyde, caught off guard, did not swing back. Instead, he doubled over to try to avoid Edward's attack. The infuriating thing is that he started laughing, even as Edward's blows continued to fly. Then, as Clyde was still bent over, Edward's right fist caught him in the right eye.

We hustled around, trying to stop Edward from fighting, when who should show up but Miss Stone herself! Why, she never came out on the playground, and here she was, just in time to witness the first fistfight of Edward's life!

"Edward!" she said sternly. "You will stay after school this afternoon! There is one thing I won't tolerate, and that is fist fighting!"

"But I couldn't stand what he was saying . . ." Edward began to protest. His mouth was screwed up like he was about to cry.

"Enough!" shouted Miss Stone. She was beginning to act angry. "I saw it with my own eyes! You attacked that young man! You will stay after school today, and that's that!"

I couldn't just stand there and not take up for my younger brother, even though I knew it wouldn't do any good. "Please, Miss Stone," I said, "please let us tell you what really happened. We all heard what Clyde was saying and he . . ."

"Oh, so you want to stay after school, too, do you?" Miss Stone whirled around and glared at me. She was shouting now. Her face was red. "Very well! That makes two of you! Anybody else want to join the group?" she yelled as she looked around the circle of frightened faces. Her nostrils flared. She was breathing so hard, her large bosom was heaving up and down. She was awfully mad.

As I stood there glaring back at her with my arm around Edward's shoulder, the funniest thought popped into my head. I was aware of the smell of talcum powder. I'll never forget that smell as long as I live!

Just as quickly as I had that fleeting thought, there was another unexpected happening. Seven-year old Fred, who had been playing somewhere else on the playground when the fight began, came running up to the group under the tree. When he saw his two siblings squared off with the unpopular teacher and heard her question, he pushed his way through to the center of the circle and said, "ME!"

He had his hands on his hips, his chin was jutted out, and he was staring Miss Stone straight in the eye. She was, obviously, taken by surprise at this bashful little boy taking such a stand. "What?" she asked Fred. "What did you say?"

"I said, 'ME!'" he answered back saucily. "You asked if anybody else wanted to stay after school, and I say YES! ME!" I could have hugged that little snaggle-toothed rascal, he was so cute standing there defending his big sister and brother.

The appearance of young Fred on the scene apparently calmed Miss Stone down. It seemed as if she almost smiled as she looked at the three of us standing together.

"Very well," she said, straightening her glasses and pulling back a strand of hair that had come loose from her bun. She stood up straight and tugged on her corset. "If that's what you want, you will all three stay after school. And that's that!" She turned to leave the scene, but stopped when she saw Clyde.

"Clyde," she ordered, "get over to the well and put some cold water on that eye. You look ridiculous!" With that, she marched back into the schoolhouse.

Like everybody else, Clyde had been standing silently during this little episode. I looked at him, then, and saw that his eye was beginning to swell. He was going to have a shiner! It was all I could do not to laugh at what Edward had done to Big Bad Clyde! He really had it coming, I thought, but who would have thought our easy-going, mild-mannered Edward would be the one to do it?

Clyde, always trying to give the impression of being important, stood up straight and tall, tilted his head back so that his sharp chin stuck out, and puffed out his chest. He put one bare foot directly behind the other, slowly turned himself around, and started walking toward the well. This was the way he always made his exit from a group, but this time he did, indeed, look ridiculous, with his eye already swollen half shut!

As we all hurried back into the building for the closing hour of school, there was a low rumble of thunder in the distance. Apparently another thunderstorm was moving our way. It sounded like a warning sign that more trouble was ahead. In spite of the warmth inside the schoolhouse, I had a shiver.

CHAPTER 6

A short time later, when Miss Stone rang the dismissal bell, the students began to leave. As we stood watching them file out of the building, I noticed Clyde, with Toby by his side, slinking away in the direction of home. His eye was swollen shut!

"Look at Clyde," I whispered to my brothers. He kept glaring back at us with his one good eye, but he didn't say a word to anybody. Edward puffed out his chest proudly for a moment. We couldn't keep from smiling—but the moment didn't last.

The rest of our friends left reluctantly. Our neighbors were the last to go. Through the open door we watched as they walked slowly across the schoolyard and down the hill, looking as sad and scared as if it were the end of the world.

As we huddled near the door, I realized that, except for the dark clouds rolling across the sky, everything else in the world was totally still. Not a thing stirred.

Then we turned to face Miss Stone. She sat at her desk on the other side of the room, looking like a sober judge about to pronounce a sentence on the guilty parties. But instead of a gavel, she held a very large switch!

She gestured for us to come to her desk. The room was as still and dark as a sepulcher. We lined up like statues in a graveyard in front of her desk. An eternity passed as we stood facing our judge, awaiting our sentence. The low rumble of thunder was like a drum roll before the pronouncement of our punishment. The judge sat there twirling the switch in her hands, looking at us over the top of her small, smudged glasses. Finally she began to speak.

"Children," she said in a low voice, "I've been thinking about this whole incident." The smell of talcum powder filled my nostrils. Outside there was a flash of lightning followed a few seconds later by a resounding boom.

Then—I couldn't believe my eyes—Miss Stone smiled! Why, she didn't appear to be angry at all!. She began to speak. "All three of you have been very well behaved the entire time I've been at Sunny Slope. I trust this has been a one-of-a-kind incident today." While she spoke, we continued to stand as still as statues on tombstones.

"I will have to write a note to your parents explaining that you were kept after school, but that is all I am going to do to you . . . ," she looked at each of us over the top of her glasses, " . . . *this time*," she added emphatically. "But from now on, I suggest you keep away from Clyde."

We just stood there, silently, not believing our good fortune. She began to write with a special pen that she kept dipping into a little bottle of black ink. She did have beautiful handwriting, with lots of swirls and curlicues. Her penmanship was one thing I had always admired about Miss Stone.

"All right, children," she actually smiled at us again. "Take this note to your parents. I feel certain I will never have to see you like this again. And that's that!" She blotted the ink with a large ink blotter, folded the note in half, and handed it to me.

"Thank you, Miss Stone," I said in a small voice. "I'll see that they get this."

"I'm sure you will," she answered. "Now hurry on home before it starts to rain. And begin working on your projects, you two." She gestured at Edward and me.

We quickly gathered our tablets and lunch pails and moved toward the door. I glanced back one more time. Miss Stone was still sitting at her desk, peering over the top of her glasses, and smiling after us.

"Thank you again, Miss Stone," I said.

"Thank you, ma'am," Edward added.

I nudged Fred. He looked up at me. I gestured with my head toward our teacher. He looked back at her and echoed our words, "Thank you, Miss Stone, ma'am."

I thought she looked pleased with herself. She nodded in our direction as we hurried out the door.

Just as we stepped outside, another flash of lightning split the clouds. The storm was closing in fast. We would have to hurry to get home before it hit.

"Whew!" Edward breathed a sigh of relief as we scurried across the schoolyard, past the well, and down the hill in the direction of home. "I never thought Miss Stone could do such a nice thing," he said.

"I'm glad she didn't use that switch on *me*," added Fred.

"Yes," I agreed, "we got off mighty easy this time, but we still have to face Mama and Papa when we get home. And that's not going to be so good." I looked at the edge of the note sticking out of my tablet before sticking the tablet and my pencil into the large pocket of my dress.

The wind was blowing very hard now. The lightning and thunder were getting closer by the minute. We ran across the countryside, scampered down the creek bank, and splashed through the creek before climbing up the bank on the other side. We only had to climb through the fence at the edge of the woods before we came out into the open area of the Singleton Field. I barely glanced at the nearby cemetery. We were almost home!

Big, fat raindrops began to fall, splattering as they landed on our heads. The smell of rain filled the air. The storm closed in around us; the raindrops pelted harder. We were running across the field when Edward slowed down a little. He yelled, "I was so relieved to hear Miss Stone say what she did about our good behavior since she's been at Sunny Sloop."

"Sunny *SLOOP*?" I laughed. We slowed down to catch our breath. "That's funny, Edward. You called our school Sunny SLOOP. I read in a book just this afternoon about large ships that are called sloops, but I never thought about Sunny Slope School being called Sunny Sloop." We all laughed about the new name for our school. We grabbed each other's hands and started running again.

The wind was so strong by this time that the tall grass swirled in all directions. We dropped our lunch pails. My hair bow took off in the wind. The lightning and thunder were constant as the sky darkened even more. It was almost as though the clouds were falling, wrapping themselves around us. Still holding hands, we ran even faster in the downpour of rain. It was frightening!

And then it happened. Just as we got to the center of the field nearest the graveyard, for some reason we all slowed down again and the three of us said the words "Sunny Sloop" at the same time. At that exact instant there was a brilliant flash of lightning that lit up the nearby tombstones like fireworks. At the same time there was a tremendous clap of thunder.

I thought we had been struck by the lightning, but instead, we were suddenly changed!

CHAPTER 7

We looked around. We were still holding hands and getting soaked to the skin, but the ground seemed to be moving. It was sloping up, pausing, then suddenly sloping back down again.

Did the lightning strike us? I wondered. Are we dead? Are we in heaven? I looked at both my brothers who were staring at me with big eyes.

There was another crash of thunder and the same action began to take place under our feet—up, up, up. It seemed as if we would fall over for a moment, so steep was the incline. Then came the pause before going back down, down, down.

Why, we were not in heaven at all! But neither were we near the graveyard in the Singleton Field. We were standing in the middle section of a large ship that was completely surrounded by water! Huge sails billowed above our heads. Sailors dashed here and there, yelling directions at each other. Some pulled on ropes, lowering sails. Others tugged on lines and cables that stretched across the deck. Everybody seemed to be hurrying. There was a feeling of panic in their actions.

As we looked around in bewilderment, the same motion began again, up and up, until we almost fell over before there was a pause, and a quick descent back down. But this time a large wave came crashing onto the deck. The powerful wave pushed us ahead of it. We grabbed each other and held on. The thunder boomed.

"What's happening?" I yelled. "Where are we?"

"You're askin' us?" Edward yelled back. We could hardly hear each other's voices, so loud was the crashing of thunder, wind, and waves. "You're the big sister! You tell us!"

"I'm afraid, Emma Mae. Hold me," Fred cried.

Just then another wave came crashing over the side of the ship. It was such a large wave that it knocked us down. We were swept across the deck in the churning water. We were about to be washed overboard when a man came running to where we were, grabbing us in his big, strong arms.

He yelled something to us, gesturing for us to go toward a cabin on the ship. We couldn't understand his words because he was speaking a language we didn't know—but we could understand his gestures. He helped us run across the wet, slippery deck.

We got to the cabin door just as another wave swirled onto the deck. The door opened and strong arms pulled us inside, into the safety of the cabin.

This time the arms belonged to, not one, but several women. They hugged us, dried us with towels, and wrapped dry blankets around us. At the same time they seemed to be chiding us.

Once again we had the feeling of not understanding their words, but knowing exactly what they were saying by their gestures and actions. We were being scolded for being out on deck during a terrible storm at sea.

The small room was so crowded there was hardly space to move. Many women, a few men, and children of all ages were huddled together, bracing each other as the ship continued to rock up and down, up and down. Some of the small children and babies were whimpering or crying.

We three sat together in a small empty space in a corner. We felt much more secure, even though the storm continued to rage outside. We had to constantly brace ourselves against the rocking motion.

I pulled Fred onto my lap. His little body was shaking, both from fear and from his cold, wet clothing. Even with the noise of the storm, I could hear his teeth chattering.

It seemed like ages passed as we huddled there, listening to the strange words being spoken around us. Finally the storm began to let up. The noise was not nearly as loud as it had been.

"Look, Freddie," I whispered. "The waves are getting smaller now. The ship's not rocking so much. Wherever we are, I think we're going to be safe."

"Where *are* we, Emma Mae?" Fred whispered.

"And what in the world are we doing here?" Edward asked.

"You know as much about this as I do," I whispered back, "but for the moment, let's just be glad we're inside with these friendly people and not out there in that terrible storm or washed overboard into the sea."

We continued to huddle in silence, taking in everything around us. The words were unfamiliar, the room rocked up and down, the smells and sounds were strange. All this mingled into a mixture of feelings we had never felt before. Our papa had a big word for what we were feeling. He would say we were "discombobulated."

As the storm moved away, the people became less agitated and began to smile as they babbled to each other in their language.

I whispered to Edward and Fred, "Seeing all these people grouped together in this ship is like looking at a picture in a history book."

"It does look like a picture," Edward agreed. "A movin', talkin' picture."

I looked down at Fred, sitting in my lap. Just as I suspected, he had fallen asleep.

"Can you figure out what language they're speaking, Ed?" I asked.

"I don't know for sure, but I think it's German," he answered. "Once in a while I hear a word or two that sounds familiar, like '*ja*' and '*nein*.'"

"I wonder why our ancestors practically stopped speaking German when they got to America," I said. "It would definitely come in handy if we knew more than just a few words or phrases right now."

"It sure would," he agreed.

We sat in silence again, listening, watching, observing.

Suddenly the door burst open and a man with a red face and a bushy brown beard came rushing in, holding a young boy of about sixteen by the back of his collar. The boy looked very frightened.

The man shouted, "*Wir fanden einen anderen Blinden passagier!*"

People gathered around them, looking at the boy. Suddenly I realized that the strangest thing had just happened. I had understood every word the man had said, even though it had been spoken in German. He had said, "We found another stowaway!"

My eyes got big with wonder. Immediately I looked at Edward. His face must have been a mirror to my own, because his eyes were also opened wide!

A woman asked, "*Sie haben einen anderen Blinden passagier?*"

I knew she had asked, "You found another stowaway?"

Edward and I stared at each other in amazement. Why, we were suddenly able to tell exactly what was being said! It was magic!

The man continued speaking in German, but we knew he was saying, "Yes, I've found another stowaway hiding in the hold of the ship where the livestock are kept! This is the second one we've found so far."

The grown-ups in the room shook their heads and frowned disapprovingly.

"We have enough mouths to feed as it is, not to mention having these stowaways to keep alive," said one of the women.

"What will we do with him?" asked another. "We barely have space for the *paying* passengers, let alone another one who has sneaked on for a free ride!"

"Lock him up with the other one," grunted someone else. "We don't owe him a thing!"

"I say, let's take him to the captain," suggested one of the older men. "If he approves, we'll tie him up in the lower deck until we get to the next port."

There was a general nodding of approval from the adults gathered around the stowaway. The boy was shaking. Each time another angry voice would speak, he would cower with his hands in front of his face.

"If he likes the livestock so well," said still another man with long gray hair, "why don't we make him stay down there in the bilge with the cattle? In that lower part of the ship he can milk the cows and clean the stalls."

"Good idea," said the large woman beside him. "He can earn his board and keep until we put him out on his own."

The bearded man with the red face spoke again. He was the one who had first brought the poor boy into the room. He was still holding him roughly by the collar. "Well, if that's what the group wants to do with him, I guess I'll go along with it. But I think if we find any more stowaways, we'll just throw them in the brig. We can't afford to keep on feeding extra mouths like this. We might even have to make them walk the gangplank!"

"Now, now, George. Let's not be too rash," another man said in a calm, kind-sounding voice. It was the tall man with a neat beard who had saved us from being washed overboard only a short time earlier. "But, come, now. It's getting late. I'll go with you to take this youngster to the captain. I think he'll agree that he can work with the cows and other livestock until we arrive in port."

"Very well, Johann," said the man with the bushy beard. "Open the door and let's get on with it."

The man named George jerked the boy around and shoved him toward the door. The person whose name was Johann, opened it, and the three of them disappeared.

Edward and I had been listening intently. We had been so fascinated with the fact that we could understand the unfamiliar language, we really hadn't thought about the meaning of the words they were actually saying. But as the door banged shut and the people began to settle down in the darkening room, something suddenly occurred to me with a shock. Why, in our situation here, we were possibly in danger ourselves! They might think *we* were stowaways!

"Ed!" I whispered in alarm, grabbing his arm. "Ed! Are we stowaways?"

Fear dawned in his eyes. "I don't know what we are, Emma Mae," he answered, "but we sure didn't pay any passage to get here."

Just then, Fred turned in my lap. I repositioned my little brother so I could cradle him protectively in my arms.

CHAPTER 8

It was then that I noticed him. I had been concentrating so hard on everything going on around us that I had not focused on individuals yet. But just as I began to think about our possibly dangerous situation, I looked up and I saw him. The first things I noticed were his eyes. They were staring straight at me.

Then I noticed that he was tall and thin. He had a sharp chin that stuck out and he had bumps on his face. He looked so much like Clyde that it instantly gave me the creeps!

As our eyes met, he turned and looked away. I knew in that one glance he was checking us out. I leaned over and whispered, "Ed, don't look now, but I think, by whatever kind of magic we came to this ship, Clyde came, too."

"What?" Edward responded. "What do you mean?"

"See that tall boy standing over near the door? The one with his hands in his pockets? I think that's Clyde. Or at least a Clyde look-alike."

Just as Edward and I both looked, he turned and glanced at us again, then looked away. He had a sneer on his face.

"Oh my goodness, Emma Mae. I see what you mean! He could pass for Clyde's twin brother," Edward agreed. "That's spooky!"

"What's spooky?" a little voice asked. Fred was waking from his nap.

"Well, actually, Freddie, this whole situation is spooky. While you were asleep, Ed and I found out a few things about our whereabouts. Like, we know we're on a ship in the open sea, and we're pretty sure the people on the ship are from Germany," I began.

Edward continued, "We found out that they don't want uninvited passengers, and there's a fellow standin' over there who looks just like Clyde."

"Now tell us, little brother, how do you like all that?" I asked him.

"I don't know if I like it or not," Fred answered, still leaning back in my arms with a puzzled look on his face.

It was getting quite dark and stuffy inside the room by now. Lanterns had been lit and hooked over pegs around the edges of the room. They swayed back and forth, back and forth, back and forth, with the rocking movement of the ship.

Suddenly, Fred sat bolt upright, grabbing his stomach with his hands. "Emma Mae?" he said in a loud whisper.

"What's wrong?"

"My stomach hurts. I think I'm going to throw up."

I felt panicky. I looked at Edward. "What are we supposed to do now?" I asked him.

"We'll have to go over and walk out that door by Clyde," Edward said, "to get him outside in the fresh air."

"I agree with you. We need to get him outside." I paused for a minute. "Besides, it's time for us to start looking around to see if we can figure out what to expect next."

Edward nodded, then said, ""Before we go out, though, Freddie, there's one more thing you need to know. We've found out that, if we listen really hard when people are talkin', we can understand what they're sayin', even though they're speakin' in another language."

"Isn't that just like magic?" I asked him.

His eyes were big with wonder. "If it's magic, then why can't we do a magic trick and go back home?" he asked.

"We haven't found the way yet, little one, but we will. Try not to worry. Sooner or later, we'll find a way to get back home."

"Emma Mae," he looked at me again with an urgent look on his face. "My stomach is really hurting!"

"All right. Let's go outside, but try to act as natural as you can," I suggested.

"Let's walk slowly, boys, slowly."

We walked nonchalantly toward the door. My heart was thumping so hard I was afraid everybody could hear it. To my surprise, nobody seemed to pay any attention to our being there. Nobody, that is, except you-know-who. Out of the corner of my eye I could tell he was watching us, all the way across the room and out the door.

When we stepped out of the hot, stuffy room, we had another big surprise. The fresh air! It was wonderful! Since the storm had passed on by, a cool, refreshing breeze was blowing, gently filling the huge sails that had been unfurled again above our heads.

It was not quite dark. We found our way across the wooden deck to a place where we could stand by the railing, in case Fred was sick. As we looked out across the water, we saw the sun making a spectacular show in the western sky.

"Just look at that," Edward exclaimed. "Is that not the most beautiful sunset you've ever seen in your life?"

The brilliant multicolored reds, pinks, and purples of the sunset were perfectly reflected in the now-smooth water, forming an upside-down sunset. It was, indeed, a breathtaking sight. For the next few minutes we stood in silence, soaking up the beauty of that moment. There was not a sign of the terrible storm that had passed over only a short time earlier.

Somewhere on deck we could hear people talking. Somebody laughed. There was also the smell of food being cooked. "You know," Edward said, "this might not be a bad place to be, after all."

"*If we were paying passengers,*" I reminded him. "We'll have to be constantly aware that we are here without permission. We mustn't forget it for a minute. And we can't let anybody else know."

Just as I said those words, out of the corner of my eye, I thought I saw a slight movement.

"That's true," Edward agreed. "We don't know what they might do if they found out."

"Don't worry about *me*," Fred reassured us. "*I* sure won't tell!"

I had to laugh at his seriousness. "I'm not worried about you, Freddie. By the way, you haven't complained about your stomach since we came outside. How are you feeling now?"

"Oh, I forgot all about it. I think I'm just hungry."

Overhead, the evening star had begun to glow. Automatically, I began to chant the rhyme which Mama had taught each of us when we were small:

"Star light, star bright, first star I see tonight,

I wish I may, I wish I might, have the wish I wish tonight."

The boys joined me in saying the simple little rhyme. We joined hands, closed our eyes tightly, and made our wishes. Then we said the rest:

"Star bright, star blue, may my wish come true."

We each kissed the thumb on our right hand, put the thumb in the palm of our left hand, made a fist with our right hand, and stamped the kiss. We smiled as we did this ritual together. It made us feel close to Mama and home.

Now, from behind us, we heard distinct sounds. People were coming out of the crowded room where they had huddled during the storm. Some of them moved in small groups along the narrow passageway toward the opposite end of the ship while others turned and walked in the direction where we stood near the lifeboats.

As we watched the people strolling along, I had the distinct feeling that *we* were the ones being watched. I looked around quickly, but there was no one in sight.

"Ed," I whispered. "How loud were we talking a minute ago when we said we were not paying passengers? Do you reckon it was loud enough to be heard a short distance away?"

"I don't think so. Why?"

"Oh, no reason." I was still whispering softly. "But in the future we need to be careful to discuss our secret in very quiet voices."

"Will do," Ed whispered back.

"I'm still hungry," Fred interrupted. He was whispering, too. "Do you think they have any food on this big boat?"

"Surely they do," I answered. "Maybe that's where the people are going . . . to eat supper."

"I could use a little food myself," Edward said. "Actually, now that you mention it, I could use a *lot* of food. I'm *really* hungry!"

"Then why don't we choose a family to follow? We can see what they do, and if we do the same things, maybe nobody will pay us any mind," I suggested.

We stood by the outer railing, watching everything around us. I looked up to see the masts with their billowing sails beautifully silhouetted against the darkening skies.

A large number of people walked along the open passageway in our direction. One family approached and walked past. For some reason all three of us, almost magically, began walking at the same time, falling in step behind that family.

As we strolled along behind them through the main body of the ship, we saw small rooms along the outer walls. They looked as though they might be living quarters for families. The first ones had curtains at their single window with a washbasin on a stand below it. There were bunks, one above the other, on either side of an open space. Trunks and small pieces of furniture crowded each room.

"These rooms look nice," I said. "They must be first class cabins for the rich people." I was glad I had studied about ships at school so I knew a little about how they were laid out.

"Our family" did not stop at any of these. Soon we were walking past rooms that were even smaller and more crowded. There were no curtains and no washbasins.

"What kind of passengers would stay here, Emma Mae?" Edward asked.

"I guess they would be second class families," I answered. "Or maybe groups of single women or single men."

But our family did not stop in any of these, either. Instead, they continued to walk until they came to an area in the middle of the ship where they turned off into a narrow passageway that led to the right. A painted sign read "Tween decks."

"What do you think that means?" Fred asked.

"I'm not sure, but I think it means just what it says—between decks. See the steep, narrow steps that look like a ladder? It's going down below to another level."

As we were discussing this, the family we were following turned. One by one, they backed down the stairs. It looked a lot like climbing down out of a hayloft. From where we stood, a short distance away, it looked pretty scary.

When they had all disappeared through the opening, Edward grinned and said, "You're the oldest, Sis. You go first."

"Make a note that I'm also the bravest," I retorted, smiling. I followed the example of the family by turning so that I could back down the steps. The boys followed right behind me. At the bottom, we found ourselves in a large room where lighted lanterns swayed at various places, giving off dim light.

It was quite crowded already as many families seemed to be sharing this large space between the decks. On one side of the area, the beds were lined up on two levels, practically end-to-end. Boxes and crates were stacked along the outer walls and in the corners.

In the other direction there were large tables. The family we were following didn't seem to pay any attention to us as we followed them to the eating area. The scrubbed wooden tables had large pots of food. The smell of fresh-baked bread filled the air.

"Look," Edward said in an excited voice. "They have square wooden plates with stakes holdin' them so they can't slide around when the ship rocks."

We watched as each person in front of us took a plate off the stack. We followed their example, moving through the line. A smiling lady put a scoop of beans and potatoes on our plates. The next woman added a slice of bread.

We sat at the end of one table in the crowded room and quickly ate our food. "Emma Mae?" Fred asked. "That tasted so good, can I lick my plate?"

I reached over and tousled his hair, smiling at him. "Now what would Mama say if you asked a question like that?"

"I think she would say, 'Now mind your manners, *junger Mann*."

"You're exactly right, young man," I said, smiling. "Why don't we just put our dirty plates on the stack like the others are doing. Then we can see why the children ahead of us are forming a line."

The children moved over to a big bucket with a dipper in it that was sitting on a shelf. Each child took the dipper and drank from it before putting it back in the bucket for the next person. We got in line, too, and took our turn.

Fred went first. He took a sip and his eyes grew big. He drank deeply before letting the dipper clatter back into the bucket. "I thought it was going to be water, but it's milk. It's yummy. It tastes just like Bossy's milk back home."

He was right. The fresh, warm cow's milk was a nice surprise! Now I knew why the pungent odor of livestock was noticeable in the room. There must be cows on the deck below us. That would be where the stowaways were being held prisoners.

Out of the corner of my eye, I kept watching our family. When they finished eating, they walked over to a space where there were two stacked beds. A hammock swung between the heads of the two beds. Immediately, the four girls climbed into one of the beds—two above and two below—and the tall boy sat down in the hammock. The father got in the upper space on the second bed while the mother lay down on the bed below him.

Other people were still coming down to eat. The person that reminded us of Clyde was among those just arriving. Once again, he glared at us through lowered eyelids.

We stood in the middle of the large space, looking around. I was sure the beds would all be filled, and I could see no other space available where we might sleep. For the first time since our arrival, a wave of fear spread over me. What were we doing here? What were we supposed to do now? How could we get away from the boy who kept staring at us?

As I stood there, unsure about what to do next, Edward whispered, "Why don't we go sit in that space in the corner?"

"Good idea, Ed," I responded. The three of us made our way to a tiny empty area in the dark corner, away from all the activity in the crowded room. We huddled together. I was relieved to see that the family we had followed was still in view from our space.

Fred said, "Look! There's a quilt wadded up over there. Maybe we can make a pillow out of it so we can go to sleep."

I patted his back. "Way to go, little Fred. That should work just fine."

He got the quilt and I helped him roll it into a long pillow. Even with our rolled-up quilt, we tossed and turned on the hard, wooden floor. We had nearly gotten situated when I realized I needed to find a toilet. The trouble was, I didn't know what girls and women were supposed to do in such situations. I kept watching our chosen family, hoping someone would lead me.

And would you believe it? Before long, two of the girls we had been watching climbed out of their bed and walked toward the ladder. One of them appeared to be a little older than myself; the other, a bit younger.

"Save my place," I told my brothers. "I need to leave for a minute, but I *hope* to be back shortly. Don't go 'way," I teased.

Both of them had sleepy-looking eyes. Neither of them smiled.

I walked quickly across the room so I could follow the girls. When I got to the ladder, I was not surprised to see the Clyde look-alike almost blocking my way. I discovered that, up close, he resembled Clyde even more. He looked at me suspiciously as I hurried up the ladder.

When I got to the top, I followed the girls along the main passageway. We hadn't gone far until we came to a place where a short line of other women and girls stood outside a closet-like room. I soon found that an appropriate container was placed inside for our use.

But the most interesting thing about this little excursion was the conversation that took place as we returned to our spot between the decks. The older of the girls turned and looked directly at me and, speaking in German, said, "I don't think I've met you before. My name is Margareta."

I had no idea how I was going to answer her. Even though, in these strange circumstances, I understood her language, how was she going to understand mine?

I knew I had to say something, though, so I answered in English. Or at least I *thought* it was English. "My name is Emma Mae," I said. But surprise of surprises! The words came out of my mouth in German! It sounded like, "*Ich heisse* Emma Mae."

"I'm very pleased to meet you, Emma Mae. This is my sister, Elisabeth," Margareta said. "We always call her Bessie."

"It's good to meet you, too," I answered. I was so amazed by the strange words coming from my lips I hardly knew what to do. Why, I was thinking in English, but speaking in German!

"What did you think of the storm this afternoon?" Margareta asked me as we strolled along.

"It was the worst storm I think I've ever been in," I said. The German words continued to flow. This is not possible, I thought. Why, I only know a few words in German! How can this be?

Before we returned to the steps, Margareta and Bessie strolled across the ship to an open space so they could look up at the sky. "Ah!" the older one said. "This is one of my favorite things about being at sea—looking at the nighttime sky."

I followed their lead, looking upward to the stars. It was dazzling—unlike anything I'd ever seen before. "Beautiful, really beautiful," I said in English. But the words sounded like "*Schon, wirklich schon.*"

We returned to the steps and went back down, single file. When I got to the bottom and started to my corner, you-know-who was still standing there with that mocking look on his face. In his eyes was a look of contempt.

I realized that for some unexplained reason, my brothers and I had an enemy on board the ship. And as I passed near him, I realized something else. Like Clyde back home, he had bad breath!

CHAPTER 9

The night was long—the longest night of my life. First of all, our clothes were still damp and stiff from the salty water that had swooped us across the deck during the afternoon thunderstorm.

Then the floor was hard. The beds were packed with people of all ages and sizes. The odor of unwashed bodies filled the air. There were both sounds and smells made by cows, chickens, and other livestock coming from the deck below us, seeping through cracks in the floor. Occasionally, a baby cried. There were people talking quietly, coughing, and after a while, snoring.

But worst of all was the cold. It had been hot and stuffy at first, but after a few hours, the cold settled in. I noticed that little Fred was shivering, so I took off my petticoat. This underskirt with ruffles on the bottom was just right to use as a blanket to cover him. I thought he had drifted off to sleep when, suddenly, he sneezed.

"*Gesundheit!*" Edward and I whispered in unison. This was one of the German words we knew in real life. Somehow, as we smiled at each other through the darkness, it brought an even stronger feeling of togetherness.

The gentle rocking of the boat never quit. I wanted to turn it off, but it just kept on and on, rocking and rocking. My stomach began to feel like it was rocking, too. I thought I was going to be sick. I tried to get my mind off it by twirling my gold necklace, but even that didn't help.

It was dark inside the room with only one dim lantern across the way that kept swaying with every movement of the ship. This made my stomach feel even worse.

"How did we get here?" I kept asking myself. "And why?"

I had no answers to these puzzling questions. Nor did I have an answer to the most important question of all: "How are we going to get back home?"

I could tell that Edward was not sleeping well, either, as he kept turning over again and again. Finally, when I felt I couldn't lie there another minute, Edward whispered, "Emma Mae, why don't we go up on deck? Maybe we can sleep better up there."

"Good idea," I whispered back. I thought we would have to wake Fred, but when I looked closely in the darkness, I saw that his eyes, too, were wide open.

I gathered up my petticoat and Edward got our quilt. The three of us quietly tiptoed across the room and up the steps.

When we reached the top, we retraced our steps back along the passageway. As we stepped out onto the main deck, we paused for a minute to look at the brilliant stars over our heads.

"Would you look at that sky!" Edward whispered in awe. "They don't make stars like that in Kentucky."

The almost-full moon was riding low in the sky. It's reflection across the water looked like a pathway of light. The combination of moonlight and starlight made it easy for us to see our way around. The cool, fresh air felt wonderful!

There were very few people sleeping out here. Edward led the way around to a part of the ship that was sheltered from the wind. Along this wall of the ship near the lifeboats, we found a place with coils of big ropes. There was also a lantern mounted to the wall, giving off a soft light.

"Why don't we try sleepin' here beside these ropes?" Edward suggested quietly. We all three lay down, staying close together for warmth. We used some of the ropes as pillows this time. That way we could use our quilt and my underskirt as cover.

My stomach felt better since we were out in the fresh air. We had just about settled down to sleep when I heard it. A movement in the ropes!

I sat straight up!

"What was that?" I asked sharply, in a loud whisper.

"What was what? Edward asked tiredly.

"I heard something," I answered, "in there!" I pointed to the ropes.

"It's just your imagination," Edward said. "Be still and try to get some sleep. I'm really tired."

"Me, too," whispered poor little Fred.

"All right," I said. "I'll try."

I was sure I wouldn't be able to get to sleep with that noise so close by. Cautiously, I lay back down and closed my eyes. The next thing I knew, the sun was shining in my face. It was dawn. We had made it through the night!

CHAPTER 10

It wasn't long until activity began to pick up on the ship. At first it was sailors and other crewmembers performing tasks. Then passengers started appearing, strolling around. The smell of food was in the air again. My stomach still felt unsettled, but as soon as the boys woke up, they were ready to get something to eat.

We made our way back down the steps to the area where we had eaten last night. The family we had been watching was already having breakfast. Big pots were set out again—this time filled with porridge.

After eating a bowl of the tasteless mush along with a piece of bread and a drink of fresh milk, we made our way back up to our space on the deck.

It was a gorgeous day. The sky was clear and deep, deep blue. The sails were filled with the brisk breeze, moving the ship quickly across the smooth water.

Edward, Fred, and I stood at the railing near the ship's stern, or back part of the ship. We watched the water foaming up behind us in the ship's wake. It reflected the blue of the sky, but with the added sparkles of sunlight dancing in the ripples like so many sprinkled diamonds. Seeing the beautiful ocean from this point of view suddenly made me want to write about it.

"I wish I had something to write on," I said. But just as I said the words, it occurred to me. I still had my tablet in my skirt pocket.

Quickly, I reached in my pocket and pulled it out. It was only slightly crumpled.

"Look, fellows," I exclaimed. "Here's my tablet with the note from Miss Stone in it. Can you believe it? I had totally forgotten about it."

Edward commented. "All of that seems like it was a hundred years ago."

"Or maybe a million," Fred added.

As I opened the notepad, my pencil rolled out onto the deck. I reached down and grabbed it before it disappeared between the cracks.

"Hey! I just had an idea," I said. "Why don't I keep a journal while we're on board the ship. We know that we're surely not here to stay, but in the meantime, I can write down everything we see and hear."

"That's a great idea," Edward agreed. "Say! Maybe you can use that as your school project when we get back to Sunny Slope."

"I like it! I like it!" I answered excitedly. "But what will I do for a date?" I asked. "Every journal begins with a date."

"You just happen to me in luck, my lady," Edward said, bowing. "While you and Fred were rollin' our quilt into that long pillow last night, I saw a book in the corner. It looked like it might be a diary of some kind. I glanced inside it. I couldn't read the German words, of course, but I *could* read the numbers on the first page that looked like a date. It said '1845/9/3.'"

"1845?" I asked. "Why, Edward, if my memory is right, that's the same year our great-grandparents sailed to America. Wouldn't that be a coincidence?"

"What's a coincidence?" asked Fred.

"Well . . . ," I began, "you tell him, Ed."

"It's like when two things happen at the same time and you can't explain why."

Fred looked very serious. "There's *lots* of things happening around here that *I* can't explain," he said, frowning.

"I know what you mean, buddy." Edward patted him on the back. "But gettin' back to your journal, Emma Mae. You can call it 'Life on board the . . .' Wait a minute. What *is* the name of this ship?"

I shrugged my shoulders. "I don't have any idea," I said. "While I'm writing, maybe you two can scout it out."

"Yes, ma'am!" Edward said. He gave me another salute. Fred imitated him. "We're off to fulfill your mission, Cap'n Em."

"Just don't stay away too long," I called as they hurried out of sight.

I looked for a place where I could sit and write. I finally found one near the lifeboats where we had slept last night. There was one small coil of ropes that was just the right height for me to use as a writing table.

I used my imagination to help fill in the details I didn't know. For instance, how long had this ship been sailing since it left Germany? From where had it started? Where was it going? Who were the people on board? How did they come to be here? And why? I had no answers to these questions, of course, and I sure wasn't about to ask!

So I made some guesses. From the size of the servings of food, the ship probably hadn't been at sea too long. The people appeared to be in good health and there seemed to be plenty of water. From the books I had read, I knew these were sometimes problems on long overseas trips.

For my journal, I would pretend that I was a real person of the time, traveling to America with my family.

Let me see. How many years ago would that have been? I scribbled at the top of the first page of my tablet. Miss Stone had taught us how to do this last year. Nineteen hundred fourteen take away eighteen hundred forty-five. That would be . . . sixty-nine years ago.

Now, how would my journal begin? If the ship set sail on September 3, and it had been sailing for eleven days, that would make today's date . . . the 14th!

And so I began my journal:

"Day Eleven at Sea—1845/9/14:

After ten days of routine life on board the ship, yesterday we had our first adventure. It was a terrible storm!"

I began to write all the descriptions I could think of about the storm we had experienced the day before. I described the food, the crowded conditions on the ship, and the spectacular sunset. I wrote about the sleeping situation, the smells, the sounds, the rocking motion, the feelings I had experienced.

I was so excited about my project that my pencil fairly flew across the page. It wasn't until I heard voices talking nearby that I was reminded of my circumstances.

Many people had gathered around the deck near midship by the tall main mast that had the crow's nest located high above. A sailor was standing on the small platform of the crow's-nest, looking out to sea. I had seen pictures of lookouts in crow's nests in my books at school, but, naturally, had never seen a real one.

From the size of the crowd it was obvious that there was about to be a meeting of some kind. The people had formed a large circle with an open space in the middle. In the center of this circle was a short man with black hair. He wore a black jacket with shiny buttons and tight-fitting white pants that disappeared into his tall black boots. From his appearance I guessed him to be a person of authority. He walked back and forth in quick, jerky movements in the middle of the open space. He kept sticking his hand inside the front of his jacket, giving the impression that he was nervous.

The way he pranced up and down the deck, speaking in his sharp crisp voice, made me think of Jiggs, our dog back home. I smiled as I recalled that, on the first day of school, Jiggs had acted just like this little man on the ship, barking out orders.

The captain, or at least I assumed he was the captain, reminded the people about the need to save on the food and water supply. He went on to say that he knew everybody would work together and that the trip would continue to be a peaceable one. There was one thing he couldn't abide, he said, and that was a passenger who couldn't get along with others.

I found it amusing that quite often the captain would pause in mid-sentence and say, "Now what was it I was going to say? Oh, yes, now I remember."

It wasn't until he made his final statement about stowaways, though, that I started paying really close attention to what he had to say. He said that the two young men who had been found on board the ship would be treated as prisoners until the ship arrived at its first port where they would be put off. In the meantime, they would have to work for their board and keep.

Then he barked out another statement. "If we find any more stowaways or other non-paying passengers, we will be forced to punish them in some way. One thing is for sure. We cannot afford to keep any illegal passengers on this ship. And that's that!"

As I stood there looking at the crowd of people, I felt very uneasy, wondering where my brothers were. I suddenly found myself looking straight into the eyes of the person who looked like Clyde. He was staring at me from across the deck with the same threatening look he had used the night before. It gave me an uneasy feeling.

The meeting was over. People began moving about, gathering together in little clusters. From across the deck, I saw two smiling boys who looked familiar. They waved at me. It occurred to me that they blended in quite well with the other children on the ship, as far as looks were concerned. All of the other boys were dressed in much the same way. Thankfully, they had worn their knickers to school yesterday instead of their overalls.

I looked down at my own dress. It was not noticeably different from the dresses worn by the other girls on board the ship. It's a good thing I hadn't worn my first-day-of-school dress. That would definitely have called attention to my presence.

As the crowd thinned out, the boys made their way back across the ship. I had started writing in my journal again.

"Emma Mae! Emma Mae!" they were practically shouting in their excitement. "We found it! We found the name of the ship!"

"Shhhh!" I cautioned as they hurried closer, putting my finger to my lips. "Not so loud. We don't want to announce to the whole crew that we don't even know the name of our ship."

"Okay," Edward said, his eyes still sparkling with excitement. "But you'll never believe it! Will she, Freddie?" He looked at our little brother.

"Never," he grinned, showing the space in his mouth where his two front teeth were missing.

"Well, don't keep me in suspense. Tell me what it is."

The boys looked at each other and snickered. "You're not goin' to believe it, Emma Mae. Not in a hundred years," Edward grinned, shaking his head.

"Not even in a million," Fred added.

"Okay, you've got me. I'm begging. *Please* tell me the name of our ship."

"You're sure you want to know?" Edward asked, prolonging the suspense just a little longer.

"*Ja*, I'm sure I want to know."

Once again the two boys looked at each other.

"You tell her, Edward. She would never believe a little boy like me," Fred said.

"All right," Edward started walking back and forth in quick, jerky movements, looking exactly like the captain had a short time earlier. He stuck his hand in the front of his shirt. He paced a few steps in one direction, then paused and walked back the other way.

"The name of the ship, my dear young lady, is . . . let me see now, what was it? Oh, yes. Now I remember. The name of the ship is . . ."

Edward was doing such a good imitation of the captain that I was doubling over with laughter. Fred was hopping up and down.

" . . . the *Sunny Sloop!*"

I stopped in mid-laugh! "You're teasing me!" I exclaimed, suddenly not amused. "Why, this is a large ship, much larger than a sloop. You're just joking, aren't you, Ed?"

"My dear," Edward continued acting like the captain, "I am reportin' to you exactly what I saw on the front of the ship. I read it with my own two eyes. The name of the ship is the *Sunny Sloop.*"

"I don't believe you. You're just making this up to tease me." I was feeling a bit annoyed.

"No, seriously, Emma Mae. That *is* the name of the ship." Edward was no longer laughing.

Fred joined in, "It is. It is. It really is. We read it on the front of the boat."

"Well," I said, beginning to believe them, "if this is true, does that have anything to do with anything?"

"Maybe, maybe not, but it sure is interestin," Edward said. "Come with us, Emma Mae, and we'll show it to you."

I tucked my notepad in my pocket and joined my brothers in a quick sprint to the bow of the ship. When we got to the front, we leaned way out over the rail so we could see the most forward part of the boat. And there it was—a large figurehead that had been carved from wood. The figure looked like a huge sun with a smile on its face. The words *SUNNY SLOOP* were carved below it.

"I think this is impossible," I said crossly, looking at the symbol with the words beneath it.

"I think it's very interestin," Edward remarked, smiling.

"I think it's magic," Fred whispered, his eyes big with wonder.

CHAPTER 11

We had just gotten settled back in our space when we heard loud voices talking nearby. On a crowded ship like this one, it was hard not to notice, so we moved over to see what was going on.

A number of people, all men, were standing in a group in an open space on the main deck. Right away I recognized some of them as people we had seen the day before in the crowded room right after the storm. They were discussing what they would be doing on their property when they arrived in America.

One man said he wanted enough land so he could start a potato farm like the one he had left behind in Germany.

Another one said quietly, "My family and I hope to get enough land to raise vegetables and start our apple and peach orchards."

Edward looked at me and asked softly, "Is that the man who saved us from washin' overboard in the storm yesterday?"

I nodded.

Still another man spoke up. I recognized him as the man with the bushy brown beard who had caught the stowaway after the storm. He said, "Trying to grow fruit in the new land is a ridiculous idea. It will be a complete waste of time. From what I understand, there is no way our fruit trees will ever grow in the new country."

The men in the group argued about a number of things, and the more they argued, the angrier they got. And the angrier they got, the louder they were. Before long, some of the men were shouting at each other. Their faces were red and they were shaking their fists.

Then one of the men looked at the man who had saved our lives yesterday and yelled, " . . . and here you are, Johann, taking up good space on this ship with all your fruit cuttings. They are probably creating a health hazard for everybody on board!"

Another man took up the complaint. "And they stink!" he yelled. "They stink to high heaven! I say we should throw them all overboard!"

"That's right," shouted the man with the brown beard. I recalled that his name was George. His face was really red now. "You're not paying extra for the space your barrel is taking up, are you?" he asked. "And what about the extra water it takes to keep them alive! We need that water for drinking!"

All the men seemed to be attacking this nice man who stood there, shaking his head in disbelief.

"I think the fruit cuttings are going to have to go!" George cried angrily. "They will never live to make fruit anyway!"

The nice man named Johann was trying to protest. "But . . . but . . . but that's going to be part of my livelihood when I get to the new world, You can't just dump it all out!"

The angry men ignored him. They stomped over to an area on the far side of the lifeboats where a barrel sat with tall twigs sticking out the top.

"Edward," I whispered, "I've heard Mama and Papa talk about how our great-grandparents started all of our fruit trees from cuttings and twigs they brought over on a ship. Isn't that right?"

"That's right," he agreed. "We know it can be done. We can't just let them throw away all those good cuttings, can we?"

"It's none of our business, Ed," I answered. "Please don't try to be a hero. Let them work it out."

By now, though, the men were so angry they began to tug on the barrel. It seemed to be their intent to dump the contents overboard.

Johann, the nice man with the soft voice, protested again. "You can't do this to me."

Still, the two men were dragging the barrel toward the side of the ship. People were moving apart, getting out of their way.

Then without warning, Edward jumped up. He looked at me in that determined way of his and said, "Emma Mae! I can't just stand here and let them get away with this. Johann was our great-grandfather's name. I don't know if this person could be related to him or not, but whoever he is, I've got to try to help him!"

Before I could open my mouth, he started running across the deck to where the two men were just about ready to hoist the barrel up onto the ship's railing.

"HALT!" Edward shouted in German! "*Das ist nicht gut!*"

The two men were so surprised to see this young boy coming after them that they did what he said. They stopped what they were doing and looked at him blankly.

"Oh, no," I whispered. "How is he ever going to get out of this without letting them know our secret?"

I grabbed Fred and pulled him in front of me protectively, gripping his shoulders with my hands.

"What is the meaning of this, boy?" asked the man with the bushy beard.

"It's just that I know . . . ah, that is . . . I *think* I know that the cuttings *will* work. I think they can make wonderful fruit in the new country."

Seeing this bold child suddenly appearing like this had caught everyone by surprise.

"You see, sir," Edward was remembering his good manners, "I just happen to know . . . I mean, I read all about it in a paper not long ago, that fruit crops do really well in America. Even though I'm just a little boy, *I* think it would be a terrible thing to throw all of these cuttings away without ever giving them a chance." All of these words were coming out of his mouth in German. It was amazing!

Other people were paying closer attention to the scene now. Most of them were nodding their heads in agreement with what Edward was saying.

"Well, we can't just let a youngster like you stop us from doing what we think is best," the bushy bearded man named George said, and he started once again to pick up the barrel.

Then he paused and looked at Edward. "As for you, young man, we'll deal with you and your impudent manner when we're finished with this job."

With that, the two men lifted the barrel so that it was now resting on top of the rail, ready to be tipped over and dumped.

I couldn't stand it any longer. I just had to get out there and assist Edward in his cause to save the cuttings. "Wait a minute, sir," I called out in German, as I dashed through the crowd that was gathering around them. Fred was at my heels. "I happen to know that what this boy says is true," I said.

Again the men stopped what they were doing and whirled around to look at me.

I went on. "In America the soil is so rich and productive that fruits of all kinds as well as vegetables grow extremely well," I was thinking fast in English, but my words were spilling out in perfect German. What an amazing feeling!

The men stood still, holding the barrel on the rail. The red-faced man stroked his beard while the other one scratched his head. They both looked puzzled.

"And how do you two know so much about farming in America?" George asked.

"Well, you see . . . ," Edward and I looked at each other, not sure what to say. Now that we had gotten ourselves into this, we had to find a safe way out. Everyone was looking at us.

Suddenly, from out of the clear blue, Fred came around and stood in front us. "We just know!" he said emphatically.

Edward and I both jerked our heads down to look at our little brother. He was standing in the same pose he had used back on the school grounds at Sunny Slope when he had stood up to Miss Stone. His hands were on his hips, his feet were planted apart, and his little chin was jutted out in a defiant manner.

"Apples and peaches and cherries and everything grows fine in Kentucky," he said.

"Kentucky? We're not going to Kentucky. We're heading for Indiana," George said.

I had begun to recover my thoughts by now, so I quickly added, "Why, of course, that's just what the information said that we were reading about, wasn't it, Ed?" I looked at Edward. He nodded in agreement.

I continued. "All along the rivers in Kentucky and Indiana there is rich, productive soil. That's why our family wants to live there."

"Whose children are you, anyway?" one of the men asked.

I knew we were in the spotlight. The crowd had moved in around us. The Clyde look-alike person was standing in the front row, taking in every word.

"We're just good little German children who are going to America with all the rest of you," I said, smiling my brightest smile. "Let's hear it for the land of opportunity! The land of freedom! Let's hear it for *America!*"

I spoke loudly, ending with my voice raised like a cheer.

"*America! America!*" Edward joined me in the chant, then Fred chimed in. To my great surprise and even greater relief, it worked. The cry was picked up by all the people who were standing in the area.

"*America! America!*" they chanted.

As Edward, Fred, and I quietly withdrew through the crowd to our own little nook by the lifeboats, we could see that George and the other man were moving the barrel back into its place on the deck. Apparently our little distraction had given their tempers a chance to cool off and they were being reasonable again. Even so, both of them still had annoyed looks on their faces. It flitted through my mind that we had possibly made enemies with them. That was the bad news. The good news was that the fruit cuttings, whoever they belonged to, had been saved for future generations!

"That was a close call," I said as we sat down on our quilt.

"You can say that again," Edward agreed, letting out a sigh of relief.

"But aren't we proud of ourselves for what we did?" I smiled. "I think Mama and Papa would have been proud of us, too."

"Yeah," Edward agreed. "I'm sure they would."

"And even our little Fred helped out. Way to go, Freddie." I pulled him onto my lap and gave him a hug.

Edward reached over and ruffled his hair, muttering, "I just hope that's the end of it. I don't know if those two men will just let it go at that or not."

"Time will tell, Ed."

"Well, that's enough about that," Edward said, bouncing back in his usual manner. "I think all that excitement calls for some lunch." He gestured toward the people who had begun to move toward the eating area. "Suddenly, I'm feeling hungry."

"Me, too," piped Fred.

"I think I'll just stay up here on deck and write," I said, "if you two think you can stay out of trouble. Maybe you can just bring me a bite to eat." My stomach still rolled occasionally with the constant ups and downs of the waves.

"Right you are!" said Edward. "Do you think we can handle the assignment, Mate Fred?"

"What's a mate?" Fred asked.

"It's a person who helps run a ship. A mate helps the captain by doin' most of the work."

"If I'm the mate, who's the captain?"

"*I AM,*" Edward and I both said at the same time. We all three looked at each other and laughed while Edward and I linked little fingers again and made our wishes.

"I guess that makes us co-captains, Cap'n Ed," I said to Edward.

"Right you are, Cap'n Em." We saluted each other.

"Okay, Mate Fred. Let's go check out the chow," Edward said, leading Fred away.

As they were walking away I heard Fred ask, "What's chow?"

"Well, it's a word that some people use when they talk about food . . ." Ed's voice grew fainter as they got farther away on their walk toward the 'tween deck ladder to go down for the noontime meal . . . never guessing what that might bring.

CHAPTER 12

It was finally quiet enough that I could resume working on my journal. I pulled my tablet and pencil from my pocket and began writing a description of the captain's speech. I had barely gotten started when I heard the sound again.

It was the same kind of sound I had heard in the wee hours of the morning. It came from down in the middle of the coil of ropes. Since it was midday, the sun was shining on the ropes. I peered inside. To my horror, I saw them. Rats! Not just one, but a bunch of them, quietly gnawing on the ropes.

Now what would we do? We thought we were so clever, finding a quiet place away from the crowds. That probably explained why most people didn't hang around out here. The place must be infested with rats. I had always heard that rats inhabit large ships, and now I knew, firsthand, that it was true.

I had also heard that rats abandon a ship that is sinking. At least they're not leaving, I thought. That should make me feel a little better.

I peeped over again and looked at the awful little creatures. Then I said, "Boo!" And, to my surprise, they totally disappeared, hiding somewhere underneath the ropes. It was as though they had not been there at all.

"I guess the secret is to keep making noises," I mumbled. "That will keep them away for a little while, at least."

I began writing in my journal again, including the part about the rats.

When the boys returned, I decided not to tell them about my discovery. I didn't know which would be worse, sleeping in that terribly crowded room below with all those people or sleeping out here where we had our own space, hoping that the rats wouldn't bother us. I would wait until bedtime to decide.

I knew from the look on Edward's face as they returned that he was unhappy about something. At the same time, Fred was smiling broadly.

"What's wrong?" I asked.

"Hardtack," Edward said in a sullen voice.

"What?"

"Just hardtack," he repeated.

"Now it's my turn to ask a question," I said, looking at my brother's gloomy face. "What's hardtack?"

"Here. Have some." Edward held out his hand. In it was a pone of hard, crusty bread. It was more like a cracker than bread.

"And that's all?" I asked.

"That's all," he said. "That and a drink of milk."

"Well, at least you had the fresh milk," I said, nibbling on the tasteless crust. "I guess this is better than nothing, but I'm really not so sure," I laughed.

Fred was still grinning. Now he began to jump up and down.

"And what's with you, Mate Fred?" I asked my younger sibling. "Did you have hardtack, too?"

"Yes, indeedy," he said, smiling broadly, "but that's not all! For all of us *little* kids they had some special pudding. I had a big bowlful. It was delicious!" He jumped up and down again.

"I'm already ready for supper," Edward grumbled.

"Not me," commented Fred. "I'm ready to run and play."

"I think that's a great idea, Freddie," I agreed. "Why don't you take a quick run around the deck? Just watch out that you don't get in anybody's way."

"Okay, Cap'n Em. Be right back," he said. And he was gone.

"Food always gives him a spurt of energy," I smiled, "especially sweets. But that's okay. He's such a good little boy, he deserves a treat."

Edward sat down on the quilt, grumbling. "But I'm a good little boy, too, and that pudding looked so good. Oh, rats!" he said.

I gave Edward a quick look to see what he meant by that last exclamation.

"It's just not fair!" he added disgustedly, propping his chin on his fists.

So he didn't know my secret, after all.

"By the way, Ed," I said, changing the subject. "My pencil needs to be sharpened. Do you have your pocketknife with you?"

I knew that Edward usually carried the special pocketknife that Papa had given him last year. Papa had said that the knife had been his own when he was a boy, and that it had belonged to his father before that. It was a very special knife, with a carved handle made of ivory.

Edward reached in the pocket of his knickers and brought out the knife. I handed him my pencil and he began to whittle it to a fresh, sharp point.

As he trimmed my pencil and I ate the rest of my hardtack, we saw two people walking in our direction. I immediately recognized the older of the two as being Johann, the man who had saved our lives and whose fruit tree cuttings we had helped save. Every time I had seen him, though, I had had this weird feeling that I had met him before. His face, and especially his eyes, looked strangely familiar to me.

I hadn't paid much attention to the younger person before. He was just a member of "our" adopted family. He was a tall, nice-looking young man with dark hair and eyes. I guessed he would be about nineteen or twenty years old. He had a spring in his step that made him look like he was bobbing up and down as he walked along.

They were both smiling as they approached the place where Edward and I sat on our quilt. They stopped right in front of us.

"*Guten Tag,*" they both said to the two of us.

We jumped to our feet.

"*Guten Tag,*" we said back to them, nodding our heads.

The older man began to speak in very rapid German, but, in spite of the quickness of his speech, we were still able to understand.

"My name is Johann. This is my son, John. We are from a place in Germany called Ottenberg, Bavaria."

Edward and I exchanged quick looks as we both drew in a sharp breath.

John joined in. "We are on our way to the place in America called Indiana. We've been told that the soil is extremely good there, just right for growing crops and orchards."

"I am pleased to meet you, Mister Johann and John," I responded, shaking their hands. "My name is Emma Mae and this is my brother, Edward." Just at that moment, as we were greeting the two men, Fred came running up to where we stood. "And this young fellow is named Frederick."

Fred reached out and shook both their hands as he had seen us do. "Glad to see you," he said, smiling his special grin. Then he looked at me and asked, "Can I please run around the boat again? Please?"

"Sure, Freddie. Go and work off some of your energy."

We watched as he sped away.

Johann went on, speaking in his deep voice. "We don't know anything about your family, but we just wanted to thank you for the part you played earlier today in helping save our tree cuttings. You must come from a fine family who has taught you good manners and who has trained you well."

"Yes, we do have a wonderful family which we hope to get back with when we get to America," I explained, "but, before we go any further, I want to thank *you* for saving us from washing overboard during the storm yesterday."

"That's right," Edward added. "We were about to be swept away, for sure."

"I don't remember seeing any of you before that happened," Johann said, "but I certainly don't know all the people on board the ship yet. I'm just glad I happened to come along before those big waves carried you out to sea."

As he said those words, he smiled. There was a twinkle in his eye. That's when it hit me! I had seen this man's portrait before! This was a younger version of the same face with twinkling eyes that I had looked at so many times at home, hanging on the wall of our parlor. It just had to be!

While the kind words he was saying about us were nice to hear, I could hardly contain my excitement about the family connection, because, by this time, I was convinced that these two men were some of our direct ancestors. The older one must be our great-grandfather, which meant the younger one would be our *grandfather*. Grandfather John! Both their tombstones are located in our family cemetery in the Singleton Field!

The more they talked, the more sure I was of the connections. There were too many familiar expressions and looks that would let it be anything else. It was a tremendous thrill for me to be able to talk with them in this way. I only wished I could tell them the rest of the story about their future, but, somehow, felt this should not be done. At least, not yet.

Young John looked at the pocketknife and pencil that Edward still held in his hands. He asked to see the knife. When Edward handed it to him, his eyes grew big. A look of surprise passed over his face. He held it out to show his father. He, too, seemed quite surprised as he looked at the knife. Then John reached into his own pocket and pulled out an identical knife.

"Why, this is amazing," he said. "I wonder how we both happen to have matching knives." Edward just grinned and shrugged his shoulders.

John asked, "Say, Edward, do you do much whittling?"

Edward shrugged his shoulders again. "No, not really. I mostly just trim pencils that need to be sharpened. Things like that."

Edward seemed nervous around John, at first, but John laughed good-naturedly, putting him at ease. He was quite handsome when he laughed. His smile seemed so familiar. Why, he looked like Papa when he smiled!

"Then let me teach you how to make something," he said. "Wood carving is a hobby of mine. I enjoy it, and it helps me pass the time, especially on a long trip like this one."

"Great!" Edward agreed. He was always anxious to learn something new.

"Come on over here," John said, "and I'll show you." He and Edward walked off together. As they walked away, I noticed that Edward was bobbing along with a spring in his step, just like John.

The two new friends found a place to sit, a little removed from us, and sat down in the sun. John produced two small chunks of wood from another pocket. He began to show Edward how to work with the wood.

Fred came running up again, out of breath from his turn around the deck. Johann looked at the two whittlers working together. Then he smiled at Fred and me.

"Well, thank you again for helping out in our behalf this morning," he said. He reached out and shook my hand. Still smiling, he patted Fred on the head. "I hope to see more of you while we're on the trip. *Danke.*"

"You're welcome," I answered in German as he turned and walked away.

I sat back down and started to write again while Fred lay on the quilt, ready now for a nap. Edward and John talked and laughed as they worked together, carving the shapes.

They worked for quite a long time. I had just about caught up in my journal when they came over to show me what they had made. I was surprised to see their work. They had each carved the likeness of a clipper ship that greatly resembled the *Sunny Sloop*. Each of the miniature ships had masts and crow's-nests. They were really quite well done. All they needed was some fabric for sails.

Both of them put their pocketknives back in their pockets and shook hands. They spoke about getting together for another lesson soon. Then, as John turned to leave, he said, "Be of good cheer." And he was gone.

I nearly told the boys about the wild conclusion I was drawing regarding the family connection with these people, but decided at the last minute to keep it to myself for a while longer.

Edward was very proud of his miniature ship. He carried it around, admiring it, before he finally put it in his pocket.

"Now I've got my school project done, too," he announced. "You're working on the story, Emma Mae, and I have the ship. We'll surely make the grade with these projects!"

"But what about *me*?" asked Fred, waking up from his short nap. "I want something to take back, too," he said.

"You don't have an assignment like we do," Edward told him.

"But I still want something to take back," he said in his stubborn, little-boy voice.

"You'll surely find something special, Freddie. Just be patient."

If only we had known what kind of keepsake he was going to get, we would have told him to forget it.

CHAPTER 13

Supper was over. We were back on deck in our private spot by the lifeboats. The wind had begun to pick up in sharp gusts, causing the ship to bob up and down. This made my stomach start its uneasy feeling again.

"There's no red in the sky tonight," Edward observed as we sat down by the ropes. We looked out at the dull gray sky where the sun was sinking below the horizon. "Wonder if that's a bad sign."

"Could be," I agreed. "Papa's always said 'Red at night, sailors' delight; red at morning, sailors' warning.'"

"Well, last night it was red and this day has been great," Edward went on, "so at least that part of it's true."

"Hey, Freddie. Why are you so quiet? Didn't you like your supper?" I asked our little brother.

"I dunno," he answered. "I just feel kinda tired."

"Well, it's probably because you're not used to sleeping on a cold, hard ship deck," I said in explanation.

Edward added, "It's not exactly like the soft featherbed mattress we're used to back home, is it?"

Fred shook his head slightly. "My stomach don't feel too good, either," he added in a quiet little voice.

"My stomach hasn't felt good for two days now. I think I have borderline seasickness. Maybe that's your problem, too," I said, ruffling his hair.

As we were talking, the two girls who spoke with me the night before came over to us. They smiled warmly.

"Since today is Wednesday, and Wednesday night is play party night, we wondered if you'd like to sit with us at the party." the older one asked.

"Sure, Margareta, we'd love to," I answered. "By the way, Margareta and Bessie, these are my two brothers, Edward and Frederick."

Fred, who doesn't like to be called by his full name, cut his eyes at me in disapproval. "But everybody just calls me 'Fred,'" he said.

Bessie, who was not much older than Fred, said, "Come on, Fred. Let's go get a front seat."

I nodded at Fred and the two of them walked off together. Then Margareta led the way for Edward and me. We walked around to midship—the large open part of the boat where the speech had been made that morning. Children of all ages were sitting on the floor in a large circle. I had no idea there were so many young people on board the ship.

Most of the adults were standing around the outside of the circle, obviously enjoying themselves as much as the children. Even "Captain Jiggs" was there, moving around in his nervous sort of way.

Sitting in the middle of the circle was a middle-aged woman. Her seat was on a platform that elevated her above everybody else. A group of musicians with a violin, an accordion, and a guitar sat behind her.

I looked more closely at the storyteller. Even in the dim light, I could see that she was wearing a beautiful blue dress that looked as though it were made of velvet. On her head was a crown. She was holding a scepter in her hand.

Strangely, this woman also looked somewhat familiar. She was on the heavy side, as Mama would say. Her hair was pulled back, away from her face. She was not especially pretty, but she had wonderful eyes that twinkled, even in the dusky light. It was the eyes that looked familiar.

Had I met this person before? I wondered.

All around the circle, lanterns bobbed with the swaying of the ship. In the growing twilight, the scene looked like a fairy tale. The queen tilted her head back, looked down her nose as though she were royalty, then lifted her scepter. Everybody grew quiet.

"Let the music and dancing begin," she called out in a loud, low-pitched voice.

At the queen's command, the musicians began playing some bright-sounding folk music. Almost immediately, the children in the circle jumped to their feet and began to dance a familiar folk dance. It was a circle dance like we had done many times at parties back home.

I could see Bessie leading Fred out into the ring of dancers. Fred wasn't smiling much, but he began to go through the steps of the dance with his new friend.

Margareta turned to Edward. "Would you care to dance?" she asked.

Edward, who had always been shy around girls, started to refuse, but Margareta got his hand and pulled him out into the circle. Edward glanced at me and shrugged his shoulders as the two of them began the dance.

As I stood there watching the enchanting scene before me, I felt someone bump me from behind. I turned quickly to see who it was. To my dismay, it was the boy we had been referring to as the Clyde-person.

"Dance with me," he ordered, taking my arm. He pulled me into the ring of dancers. Not wanting to make a scene, I followed his lead. We got in step with the other dancers.

I couldn't believe it! After all those suspicious-looking stares he had given us, now he showed up to dance with me. We danced the first few minutes in silence. I kept looking for Edward, hoping he would come to my rescue, but I couldn't see him.

Finally, my partner spoke again. "Everybody calls me Tater," he grunted. Up close like this I was again aware of his bad breath. I could clearly see the bumps on his face. "What's your name?" he asked.

I really didn't want to talk to him at all. What could I say? What could I do? I was thinking hard, but could come up with nothing. So that's just what I said. Nothing.

"What's the matter with you? Cat got your tongue?" he asked shortly. I couldn't believe how much he sounded like Clyde!

I just smiled slightly and sort of shook my head. I dropped my eyes as though I were shy and blinked them.

"Look," Tater said. "I don't mean to be nosy or nothing, but I just want to know where you and your brothers came from and what you're doin' here on this boat."

Again I hung my head, shaking it slightly, fluttering my eyelashes.

"So you don't want to talk to me. Well, let me just warn you, right here and now. If you know what's good for you, you'll watch your step."

I looked down at my feet, watching them as they went through the routine of the folk dance.

"I don't mean your dance step," Tater grumbled. "I mean your way of livin'. I think you're here illegally, and I aim to prove it. I just thought I'd give you a chance to defend yourself."

This time I raised my eyes and met his, straight on. I narrowed them in such a way that I hoped he would get the message I was sending. My eyes were saying, "You wouldn't dare!"

But Tater wasn't discouraged. He muttered one more warning in a threatening voice. "I'll tell you one more time. Just watch your step!" Then he stopped dancing abruptly. At that precise moment, the music stopped.

I looked around me at all the other people. They were laughing and clapping their hands happily. When I looked back to where Tater had been standing, he was gone!

The rest of our little group came back to where I stood and we all sat together on the deck of the ship. The queen turned out to be a storyteller. She told two fairy tales, using many voices and props. She was wonderful! The entire time I kept asking myself why she looked so familiar. And why her actions and gestures reminded me of someone.

After the stories, a group of singers took the stage. They did funny acts along with their music. At the end of the program, there was another group dance.

The full moon overhead seemed to be dancing, too, or playing hide-and-seek with the clouds. The water with its choppy waves sparkled in the moonlight as far as you could see. The whole world seemed to be reflecting the happy mood of the people on the ship at that moment.

By the time the music ended, it was getting quite late. Margareta came over and took Elisabeth by the hand.

"Time for us to go," she said. Then she looked at her little sister more closely. "Why, Bessie, what's wrong? You don't look like you feel well."

"My stomach hurts," the little girl answered. "I think I danced too much."

"Maybe you just need to get to bed," Margareta said, putting her arm around Bessie's shoulders. The two girls turned to look at us. "See you soon." They waved good-bye.

"*Gute Nacht,*" we all said to each other. They walked down the passageway toward the steps that would lead to the large room below where their family slept.

Edward and Fred were ready to go to sleep, too.

I had been so caught up in the entertainment of the evening I had not had time to worry about Tater and his unpleasant warning. I decided that the news about the rats and Tater could wait until morning.

We pulled our quilt from its hiding place and got ready for bed.

Fred looked especially tired. When I gave him his good night kiss, I thought his face felt warm. I put my hand on his forehead, the way Mama always does, to see if he had fever. He did feel a little warmer than usual, but I thought it was because of the excitement of the evening and the dancing.

The three of us lay close together for warmth. I took off my petticoat to use for extra cover again, and we all lay down to sleep.

"Emma Mae," Fred said in his sleepy, little-boy voice. "Can we say our bedtime prayer now?"

"Why, sure, Freddie. I'm sorry I almost forgot. I'm glad you reminded me." The three of us said: "Now I lay me down to sleep, I pray thee, Lord, my soul to keep. If I should die before I wake, I pray thee, Lord, my soul to take. Amen."

By the time we had finished, Fred's eyes were closed. Within a matter of minutes, Edward, too, was breathing deeply. I was the only one who lay awake, twirling my gold necklace and peering at the round moon as it continued its fairy-like dance across the sky. But even with the boys snoozing away, there were a number of reasons why I couldn't get to sleep.

One, my stomach was once again rocking uneasily with the choppy, swaying motion of the ship as the waves had gotten larger. Two, my memory was replaying the encounter with Tater over and over again. But the third reason was the main one. I was listening . . . listening . . . listening for the sound I was sure would come. The sound in the ropes.

CHAPTER 14

It seemed as though I had lain there for hours before I heard it, but it finally happened. My heart sank. Yes, it was the same sound I had heard last night, except this time I knew what it was. It was the rats, crawling and gnawing among the ropes.

I sat up again, trying not to disturb the boys; but as I looked around me on the moonlit deck, I noticed something very strange. This can't be happening! It was not possible, but it was true! Right before my eyes, my brothers were shrinking in size!

What other weird thing is going to happen to us? I wondered! I looked down at my own body, knowing before I looked that I, too, was shrinking.

It was then that I saw him. An overweight rat peered out from between the ropes. And the strangest thing! It had eyes that glowed like two burning coals from Papa's coal-burning stove back home.

"Go away," I whispered to the rat. The rat and I, by now, were about the same size.

"Scram, get out, shoo!" These were all words I had heard Mama say to unwanted creatures. "*Geh weg*! Go away!"

Then, to my surprise, the rat began to speak. Not only was it speaking, but it was speaking in German!

Once again I had the strange sensation of being able to understand the words.

In a squeaky voice the angry rat asked, "Why should I go away?" He looked first at me and then at my brothers. "I was here a long time before you and these other two creatures came along."

At just that moment, another rat crawled out of the coil of ropes. He, too, had eyes that glowed in the darkness. "What's going on out here?" he squeaked in German. When he asked that question, a third rat appeared, and a fourth and a fifth. All of them huddled together, looking at me with their terrible glowing eyes.

I wanted to wake Edward and Fred, but I didn't know what to do. They seemed to be sleeping so soundly.

"All I know is that there are some two-legged creatures who have barged into our territory," growled the first rat, "and I don't like it at all." As he spoke, his eyes seemed to glow brighter.

"Look," I said in my unfamiliar German words. "My brothers and I didn't know this was your territory, but if you'll let me, I will wake them up and we'll leave. Just give us a break, please."

"Why should we give you a break?" asked another of the rats. It seemed that every time one of them spoke, its eyes got brighter. "What kind of a break has a human being ever given a rat, I want to know?"

"Well, don't blame me for all humans, for goodness sake!" I said. "I've never had a chance to relate to a rat before, one way or another."

"That's no excuse!" cried still another rat with particularly bright eyes. They were so bright they seemed to be almost white. His voice was so loud he woke both Edward and Fred. They sat up, rubbing their eyes and looking puzzled.

I moved over between them as they stood up, putting an arm around each of them.

"What's the matter, Emma Mae?" Edward asked. "What's happenin'?"

"You're trespassing on our ropes, that's what's happenin'," said the first rat. His eyes glowed still brighter.

"Hey, man!" another rat came running along the railing of the ship. "Did I hear my cue? Did I hear somebody ask 'What's happenin'?' That's s'posed to be *my* line!"

All three of us turned to look at this new arrival on the scene. We saw a rather plump rat plodding along. The hair on top of his head was parted in the middle, much like the hair of many of the young men and boys on the ship. But instead of having eyes that glowed like the others, this one was wearing dark glasses.

The other rats looked at the newcomer disgustedly. It was obvious they didn't want to be bothered by him.

"Get out of here, Harry," one of them said. "This is our problem, not yours."

"Hey, man. Any problem of yours is a problem of mine. We're all in this together, know what I mean?" the newcomer said.

The first rat rolled his eyes, shook his head, and sighed.

"All right then, Harry," he said. "We have some very small but unwanted creatures here in the middle of our territory, and we are in the process of deciding what to do with them."

"Have any of you thought about eating them?" one of the rats asked.

"I dunno," said another. "They don't look too tasty to me."

All at once the rat with the dark glasses cried out. As he began to speak, or rather, squeak, he suddenly looked familiar. He had a sneer on his face that reminded me of Tater.

"I've got it, man!" he squeaked. "I recognize these little people! I've seen them before!" He was so excited that the light in his eyes was glowing through the dark glasses.

"They're stowaways!" he said, getting excited. "I overheard them talking yesterday and they admitted they are not paying passengers!"

"Are you sure about this, Harry?" asked the first rat, now looking at us with disgust. "Because, you know what the unwritten law is, even for rats. All passengers without permission to sail must walk the gangplank."

"That's what I've been wanting to say," replied the rat with the extra bright eyes. "Let's make them walk the gangplank!"

One of the rats pulled out a single strand of rope that had been gnawed off from the big coils. He walked behind us. "I'll tie their hands behind their backs," he said.

"Wait a minute! Wait a minute! Just hold everything!" I cried out emphatically. "You can't make us walk the gangplank without a proper trial!"

"Says who?" asked Harry. "This is our ship and we can do as we please!"

"I'm sorry, gentlemen," I went on, "but this is just not the way it's done. I've read about it in books. There is always a trial."

"I dunno," Harry said. "What do you think, fellows? Do we do a trial or don't we?"

One of the other rats spoke up. His eyes were glowing like two huge moonbeams. "Naw," he said. "It's taking too much of our time. I'm hungry. I say let's dump them and get it over with so we can get on with business as usual."

There was a bright glow of light as the others all agreed. The rat with the rope went behind us again. This time he tied our hands behind our backs.

I just stood there, feeling helpless. Both Edward and Fred were standing so still I wondered if they had fallen back to sleep.

Two rats came running up to the group. They were carrying a small board. "Will this do?" they asked. "We've never seen a gangplank before."

I couldn't stand it any longer. I had to make another protest.

"If you've never made anybody walk the gangplank before, then why start now? We are really nice little people. We don't mean to do you any harm. All we want is a chance to get back home to our family in Kentucky." I had started to cry now. "I'm begging you," I cried. "Please don't go through with this. Please give us another chance."

The rats' eyes were all dim now. I felt sure that meant they were listening.

I looked at Edward. "You tell them, Ed." I sobbed. "Tell them how much we want to go back home. Tell them, Ed!" I was crying hard by now.

Edward turned and looked at me. To my horror, I saw his eyes were gleaming like the rats.

"It's too late, Emma Mae," he said, "too late."

I started to cry even harder. I looked at Fred, my sweet little brother. He turned his head and looked up at me. The glow was beginning in his eyes, too. "I'm so thirsty," he said. "All I want is a drink of water."

I was really sobbing now. The rats were leading us out on the little board—out over the ship's railing. The waves were rocking up higher and higher, as though they were reaching up for us.

"This is not making any sense," I called out. "Stop it! Stop it! You can't do this to us!"

They were forcing all three of us to walk out onto the bouncing board! As we bobbed up and down, the waves grasped at our feet, pulling us, tugging us, begging us to come down into our watery grave!

Slowly we moved to the end of the gangplank. We had one more step to go before we fell.

Why must we have to die so soon? I thought. And why is the light so bright?

I looked back one last time at the row of rats. Harry was the main one. He was smiling his terrible, smirky smile. All the rats' eyes were gleaming brightly. The light was so brilliant it hurt my eyes!

Just as we were falling off the edge, I heard Edward say, "Emma Mae! Emma Mae! Wake up! You're having a bad dream!"

"What?"

"You must be having a nightmare," Edward said, gently shaking me awake.

I sat up quickly and looked around. I was trembling with fear. My face was wet with tears.

I glanced up at the sky. The full moon was shining brightly in my eyes. I looked around again. Edward was right there beside me, holding my hand. We were our normal size! Fred was still asleep with his head on the ropes. He was mumbling quietly, "So thirsty. So thirsty."

"Oh, Edward! Edward!" I sobbed. "It was so terrible!" I grabbed him in my arms. He hugged me back.

"It's okay, Emma Mae. We're all okay," he said gently.

"I think I'm going to be sick!" I jumped up and ran to the rail. Edward ran along and stood beside me with his arm around my shoulders. I had never been so violently sick in my entire life!

When I felt better, we sat back down in our spot. "Whew!" I said. "If that's what it's like to be seasick, I hope I never have to experience it again."

"I guess that's what caused you to have your nightmare," Edward said, reassuring me. I nodded. Then I heard Fred mumble the words again which he had said in my terrible dream. "I'm so thirsty. All I want is a drink of water."

I reached over and touched him. His little face was so hot it burned my fingers!

"Oh, Ed!" I cried. "He's burning up with fever! What are we going to do? When is all this going to end?"

"So thirsty," Fred whimpered. "So thirsty."

CHAPTER 15

The next few hours were like another nightmare, except this one was actually happening. When Edward went running to the water barrel to get some water for Fred, he found that he wasn't the only one hurrying to get water for a sick child. There were many people there for the same reason.

He came back with a cup of water, but also with the news that there was an epidemic of some kind going around among the children on the ship. He had found out that Elisabeth and her younger sister Katarina were sick, too.

Since we didn't have anything to dip in the water, I tore a piece of material off my petticoat. I used it as a cloth to bathe Fred's face and body like I had seen Mama do when we were sick at home. But instead of getting better, he seemed to be getting hotter and hotter.

"Edward, we've got to do something," I said. "Do you know if this ship has a doctor?"

"I'm sure it does," he answered. "I'll go see if I can find out anything."

He was gone for what seemed an eternity. Fred was saying strange things. He was having chills, then cold sweats. And then the vomiting started.

It was different from the way I had been a short time earlier. I was sure this wasn't seasickness. I didn't know what to do except to bathe him, say comforting things to him, and hold him at the rail when he was sick.

And in between all this, he kept asking me to sing.

When Edward finally returned, he had a tall man with him. The man had a small black beard and wore glasses. In his hand was a black bag.

"Emma Mae," Edward said quietly, "this is Dr. Holt."

"Oh," I cried in relief. "I am so glad to see you. Our brother is a very sick little boy. We don't know what to do for him."

The doctor explained that there was some kind of strange illness that had suddenly spread throughout the ship, attacking only small children.

"Tell me, did your brother eat any of the pudding that was served at lunch today?" he asked.

I looked at Edward.

"Yes, sir, he did," Edward replied. "He was proud that he got dessert when Emma Mae and I didn't get any. He even wanted seconds, but I wouldn't let him."

The doctor shook his head. "From what I've learned, every child who ate the pudding has a very bad case of food poisoning. There is little I can do to help at this point except to give him some medicine to control the nausea a little."

The doctor rubbed Fred's limp hand and patted his hot head. He looked at me over the top of his glasses.

"You've been doing all the right things, young lady. Just keep on doing the same things until morning. I'll check back with you later."

The doctor stood up to his full height and looked around.

"By the way," he asked, "where are your parents? Why aren't they here taking care of this sick child?"

Edward and I looked at each other. I knew this question would be asked sooner or later, so I was prepared with my answer.

"Well, sir, our parents had an opportunity to come, I mean, go to America quite some time ago. They have already gotten some property and have built a house. Now we are on our way to join them."

I glanced at Edward. He smiled slightly and barely nodded his head

"Is there no one on the ship, then, to help take care of you?" Dr. Holt asked.

"Well, there's one family who's been looking out for us. It's a man named Johann and his son, John."

"Oh, yes. I know the ones you mean. I'll see if they can help, although two of their children are sick, too."

"Dr. Holt?" I looked up at him as he turned to leave. Fred had started to moan again and was getting agitated. "Is our Freddie going to be all right?"

The doctor paused before answering. Then he said in a low and serious voice, "I honestly don't know, my dear. We can only hope for the best, but, at this point, I honestly don't know."

He stayed with us a little longer while Fred was sick again, holding him at the rail and stroking his face with the wet cloth. He said kind, reassuring words. When it was over, he gave him a small dose of the medicine that we hoped would help control the nausea.

"Try to keep him sipping water so he won't get too dried out," he said. He left to see about the other children.

During the remainder of the night Edward and I took turns getting water, bathing Fred's face and body, holding him to the rail when he was sick, urging him to sip the water, and singing to him softly.

He also wanted us to "tickle" his arms, face, and body. We let our fingers trace lightly over his skin. Each time we would stop singing, he would whisper, "Sing." Or when we stopped tickling he would say, "Tickle." We quietly sang all the songs we could think of, even

Christmas songs. And we thought our arms would drop off from the constant movement of "tickling."

When dawn finally started lighting the sky, I looked at Edward, who was leaning back against the ropes, totally exhausted. "I thought our first night on board ship was the longest night of my life," I said, "but this one has been a whole lot longer."

With the new day, however, came new worries. Edward came back from the water barrel with the report that one of the little boys was near death. There was fear that he and possibly others might not pull through this life-threatening illness.

"Oh, no," I cried, holding Fred even closer in my arms. "We can't let him die, we just can't!" Tears of frustration ran down my cheeks.

It wasn't long before Dr. Holt returned. This time another man was with him. He wore a long black coat, black shirt and pants, and a black hat. He was carrying a large Bible in his hand.

"My children," he said gently, "my name is Reverend Paetznick. I understand that you are traveling alone and that your parents have preceded you to America. While I don't understand all the circumstances, I admire you for what you are doing with your little brother. I'd like to offer a prayer for his recovery."

I sat still, holding Fred's limp little body in my arms. Tears dropped onto the top of his head. His breathing was shallow and quick which meant that the fever was still with him.

The minister placed a hand on Fred's head while he prayed. Before they left, the doctor handed me another small glass bottle of medicine.

It wasn't long before we had other visitors. This time it was Johann and John. Walking between them was a woman. As they came closer, I realized that this person had been the storyteller the night before. But here in the light of dawn, standing beside her husband, I knew who she was. She was the woman beside Johann in the family portrait in my parents' home. This kind-looking person with the wonderful, twinkling eyes had to be my great-grandmother!

They talked in hushed voices, as grownups always do when there is a sick person around. The woman sat down on one of the coils of rope, then lifted Fred onto her lap. "I'll take care of your little brother for a while. You two need to take a break," she said softly.

"Here," Johann said. "We have brought some broth for the little one, and milk and bread for the two of you. You have been through a long night and you need nourishment."

While Fred sipped the broth, Ed and I gladly accepted the refreshments they had brought. John sat down between us while we ate. He placed a hand on each of our shoulders. "I think you have met two of my sisters, Margareta and Bessie, but I'm not sure you've met the younger ones, Katarina and Nellie."

"We've seen your whole family from a distance but we haven't actually met the others yet," Edward replied.

John nodded. "That's what I thought. Two of my younger sisters, Bessie and Katarina, both ate some of the pudding for lunch yesterday and have been very sick overnight, much like young Frederick here."

Johann, who was sitting beside his wife and offering the broth to Fred, spoke up. "Our youngest little girl, Nellie, decided to skip dessert yesterday, for some reason. But the other two weren't so lucky."

"Are they going to be all right?" I asked.

"Yes, thank God," answered the mother. "They both seem to be out of danger now, as I think your little Fred is, too."

Johann stood up. "I'll just go on back and check on the girls. Margareta has been watching them while we came here, but she, too, needs to rest."

They had brought more quilts. Edward and I gladly accepted them before we curled up and fell asleep in our spot by the coils of ropes. It was a wonderful relief to have such kind and loving people with us.

When we woke up some time later, Fred was still sitting in the woman's lap but he was smiling weakly. In his hand he held a small wooden cross. I looked around and saw John, who was also smiling. His pocketknife was in his hand. On the floor by his feet were curly wooden shavings. He had made the cross especially for our Fred.

The mother, now seeing us refreshed, rose to leave for a while. As she and John started to walk away, he turned back and said, "Take courage, young friends. Try not to worry. Be of good cheer."

Later, when the doctor came by to check on Fred, he looked at Edward. "You know, young man, you may have saved your little brother's life by not letting him take seconds of the pudding yesterday. There were fourteen children who had food poisoning from eating the spoiled pudding. It appears now that all the children are going to be okay. We are greatly relieved."

"Thank you, Dr. Holt, for helping take care of our Fred," I said. He nodded his head, smiling kindly, before he walked away.

John and his mother came back to check on us frequently.

The next morning the mother brought a small chain with her. "I've noticed, Fred, that the wooden cross John made seems to be special to you. Here, let me put it on this chain so you can wear it and not worry about losing it." She screwed a small screw into the top of the cross and placed the cross on the chain before hanging it around his neck. She kissed the top of his head, smiling, before she turned to leave.

"*Das ist gute*, Freddie. Now you have something to take with you when we go back home," I said.

If we ever find a way to go back home, I thought.

Chapter 16

On the Monday following the food poisoning scare, there was another new development on board the ship. School started. To my great delight, a young woman named *Fraulein* Rosamunde had been commissioned to start lessons for children of all ages. The classes, we learned, were to be held in the area of the ship called the quarterdeck, the part of the ship's deck that is set aside by the captain for special functions.

Not only would this be a great chance for us to truly learn some German words, but it would also be an opportunity for us to keep up our math and other skills. The *Fraulein* explained that classes would meet every weekday morning, except for those times when the hatches would have to be closed because of rain or when heavy seas lurched everything about. We knew that on days like that, we could stay below in the lower deck with John and his family.

One afternoon we sat in our own space after class, reviewing our multiplication tables. I asked Edward how much 9 x 9 equals. Instead of giving me the answer, he looked at me and asked, "Have you ever noticed the girl who always wears a red scarf on her head?"

"I've noticed a girl like that who's about my age. She pretty much keeps to herself. I've never seen her smile or talk to anybody or anything. Is that the girl you mean?"

"Yep. That's the one I'm talkin' about," he replied. "I've been watchin' her lately, too, and I think she's worried about something."

"Worried? Why do you think that?"

"She keeps lookin' over her shoulder, like she's afraid she's goin' to get caught. If you ask me, something's goin' on with her."

"You and your big imagination, Edward. There's probably nothing in the world wrong with the girl. Maybe she's just shy."

"You're probably right, Sis. I hope so. But there's one more thing I've noticed that adds a question mark to the girl with the red scarf—and that's the older man who is usually with her."

"You've got me again, Edward," I said. "What about the older man? Why don't you tell me the whole story?"

"Ever since I started paying attention to them, I've noticed they are always at any programs or meetings that are going on. The man wears a red scarf around his neck, a lot like the one the girl wears on her head. The strange part is, she's never there with him while the program's goin' on."

"She's never at the programs or meetings?" I asked.

"Nope. She arrives with him at first, but then disappears. He always stays there alone. He never joins in with anything that's happenin', either. Strange thing is, he keeps lookin' over his shoulder like he's nervous about something. It's probably just my imagination. All the same, I'm goin' to be on the lookout to see if there's anything strange goin' on with them."

"Why don't you do that, Detective Edward? I'll be glad to hear any other report of suspicious behavior from the red scarf people."

"Good," Ed replied, "'cause I have one more tidbit of suspicion to share."

"All right. While we're at it, share away."

"It's like this, see. The first time I noticed anything strange was one Sunday morning after worship. Bessie and I were on our way between decks for dinner with the family. It just so happened that the girl walked up to the man just as we were passin' near them. He spoke to her in English."

"English? I thought they were from Germany."

"So did I, but I know what I heard. The man smiled at her and asked, 'How did ye do, me lass?'"

"She answered, also in English, 'Great! I hit the jackpot today.'"

"He said, 'Good girl,' and gave her a hug."

"Hmmm," I said. "That is quite a tall tale, me boy. We need to keep an eye on them to see if anything else suspicious happens. Now, can you tell me what 9 x 9 equals?"

Edward laughed and said, "I thought if I told you all those stories, I'd get your mind off the multiplication tables. But if you really want to know, the answer is *einundachtzig*, or eighty-one."

"Right you are. In both languages!" I responded, smiling. We both stood and strethed, marking the end of our study session.

One day not long after that discussion, as we were sailing along at a good speed, a little darkness showed up on the horizon. Sailors appeared from all around the ship, holding onto ropes as they looked up at the sails and out to the sea. They were prepared, in case they needed to haul the sails down quickly. Suddenly, the darkness closed in around the *Sunny Sloop*, and, almost before we were able to get down to the 'tween decks level, the storm hit.

The ship lurched up and down in the storm-tossed sea . . . and so did the occupants. It was a long, miserable night with babies crying and many people dealing with seasickness. It reminded me of the storm that had first brought us to this unusual situation.

Finally, the day dawned and we were able to return to our own space on deck. With the fresh, clean breeze and fluffy clouds, there was not a trace of yesterday's storm.

The next couple of days were routine. We spent a lot of time with John, talking about many different things. I wrote in my journal whenever I had a chance. The new tablet I had taken to Sunny Slope on the first day of school was filling up fast. Thanks to John, Edward was becoming quite good at wood carving by now. And Fred kept himself occupied by just being Fred.

John's parents and his four younger sisters had also taken us under their wing, as Mama would have said. They often came by to talk with us and pass the time. It was hard not to tell them our secret, but Edward and I both agreed it was best not to get into something that was impossible to explain.

Then, one beautiful sunlit afternoon, the mother, Mary Katherine, decided to show me their big trunk that was between their bunks. She said she wanted to share about some of the things they had stuffed in it before they left their home in Germany. They wanted to have these special treasures with them when they got to America.

My heart skipped a beat when I saw the trunk. It had an engraving on it that looked like a cross in the middle of a flower garden. Before I even had time to think about what I was saying, the words just popped out of my mouth. "Why, there's a trunk that looks exactly like this sitting in a corner of our home in Kentucky."

Mary Katherine jerked her head around, looking at me with big eyes.

She opened the trunk so I could see what was inside.

"Oh-my-goodness," I exclaimed as I picked up some jewelry. "This brooch is just like one that Mama wears. And this ruby ring belongs to my Aunt Kate."

Mary Katherine still gaped at me, not saying a word. Just staring.

"And your blue velvet dress. Up close like this I can tell that it looks exactly like the one I wore to a Halloween party one night. My parents told me that it had belonged to a person who . . . dressed like a queen . . . and who told wonderful fairy tales."

By now my eyes, too, were as big as saucers. We were staring at each other in silence. Then I said softly, "This is exactly the same dress that is hanging in my Mama's closet at home!"

Mary Katherine shook her head, looking at me in amazement. Then she began to speak, very slowly. "Child, are you telling me that . . ."

"Yes," I whispered. "For some reason we have come here from your future; not because we asked to come, but just because it happened."

Once again she shook her head. "I think you need to start at the very beginning, but we'd better get the rest of the family. This is one story they would never believe, even if it came from me."

Quickly she gathered everyone together. We went topside where we sat in a group in our space on the deck and talked in quiet voices so no one else would hear. The family sat in silence, entranced by the story that Edward, Fred, and I were finally able to share.

First, we explained what we knew about what was going to happen to them when they arrived in the Port of New Orleans. The families from Bavaria, Germany, would start up the system of rivers on flat boats, headed toward their destination in Indiana. We explained how ice floes in the Tennessee River would create an ice jam that would force them to stop in Kentucky for the winter.

I said, "We've heard the story about these ancestors many times. After spending the winter in the hills of West Kentucky, they discovered that their fruit cuttings thrived there. They decided to make their homes in that area, so they managed to get land."

Johann interrupted our story. "So that's why you were so determined to save our cuttings from being pitched overboard."

Edward nodded before going on. "We've been told how the land was cleared and cabins and barns were built." He scratched his head, remembering. "The earliest folks to live there—that would be all of you—started farms and orchards."

"Another thing we've heard is how these first families were some of the founders of the Lutheran church," I said, looking at Johann. "I've even heard Papa say that his grandfather—that would be you—was one of the first twenty-one adults to be what he called a 'founding father' of the church."

"That's right," Edward chimed in. "And I've heard Mama tell how they met for church in people's homes for a long time. After a while they were able to build a church building only a few miles from our house. For a long time it was a German-speaking church."

Fred chimed in, "But we don't say words in German at church any more. We just talk in American."

The family chuckled at his remark, but most of the time they sat in silence, absorbing what we were saying. They looked from us to each other occasionally, smiling or with puzzled looks on their faces. At first they appeared to be totally disbelieving . . . and yet there was no other explanation of how we had come to know things about them or that we told them about our present life in Kentucky.

Finally, Johann began to speak. "This is all unbelievable information you are sharing with us, children, but what can you tell us about our family life?"

"We actually don't know a lot about that, I'm afraid," I said. "Since our great-grandparents and even our grandparents died before we were born, we don't really know much about their personal lives. We only know that all their graves are in the family cemetery near our home." I went to him and gave him a hug. "I wish we could tell you more."

He returned my hug and patted my back. "That's all right, my little *Fraulein*. Don't fret about it."

My brothers and I burst into laughter when he said that. The others looked at us with question marks in their eyes.

"That sounded just like our Papa," Edward explained. "At suppertime the night before we came here, Papa said those exact words to Emma Mae. She had just apologized for a remark she had made earlier, and Papa said, 'That's all right, my little *Fraulein*. Don't fret about it.'"

"How well I remember that," I laughed. "I had just commented about how much one of the students at our one-room school annoyed me because he was such a bully. Then I realized I had broken a family rule. Papa had always said, 'If you can't say something good about somebody, don't say anything at all.'"

There was a gasp from the members of the family. "Why, that's what you say, Papa," Margareta said. We all smiled at the similarities between their family and ours.

John said, "Changing the subject, Emma Mae, but I'm curious about something. Who was it you were talking about at supper that night that was not so good?"

The three of us looked at each other and exchanged smiles. "It was Clyde, the Sunny Slope bully," I said. "He looks and acts just like Tater. The two of them could be twins."

"So that's why you've been so interested in our Tater," John said. "He must be related to somebody you know in your present life. Now I understand."

"I have one more question before we break this up and get ready for supper," Mary Katherine said. "If you could name one thing that stands out in your minds about what you've heard regarding your ancestors, what would it be?"

"That's easy," I said immediately. "Papa says that when you changed your country, you changed your hearts."

Johann and Mary Katherine exchanged looks with each other, nodding their heads and smiling.

Edward's response to the question was, "John, even though we never knew you in person, we know a lot about you. You're goin' to marry a woman named Annie Kate. You'll grow up to be a doctor who writes a medical journal and invents cherry bark cough medicine. Mama told us that you did that."

John nodded, smiling broadly. "And what about you, young Fred? What can you tell us?"

Fred looked at John and grinned his snaggle-toothed grin. "Someday you're going to be a grandpa and have seven grandchildren.

You're lucky, though, because the best three of them are sitting right here in front of you."

When 19-year old John suddenly realized that, in time, he actually *would* be our grandfather, he raised his hands above his head and, looking skyward, asked, "Lord, what have I done to be punished by having these three rascals for grandchildren?"

There was loud laughter from the entire family group. Since it was time to go for supper, we reached out and formed a circle that was followed by the biggest group hug that had ever been done on board the *Sunny Sloop*. Along with the tears and smiles, it was a moment I knew I would never forget.

Following the hard-to-be-believed story, our life together on board the ship entered into a new phase. For instance, our great-grandmother told fairy tales again, but this time they were just for us. We shared stories about home life on both sides of the ocean. It was a wonderful time.

One day, during another rough day at sea, we crowded together in their space on the lower deck. To help get our minds off the terrible ups and downs of the ship, we sang for them. We sang some of the songs we had learned at church and school, but also some songs that we knew which were American songs. They loved hearing us sing.

That night, because of the awful conditions above board, they let us sleep in the space between their beds. Before Mary Katherine got in her bunk, she gave each of us a warm, tight hug. "I'm so glad that, by whatever way you came to be here, we are having this chance to get to know you," she said softly. "You have come to be very special to us all."

"Yes," I replied softly. "We feel the same way about all of you. You're a wonderful family, just like I knew you would be."

Edward added, "I'm so glad we could f-i-i-i-n-d you . . . f-i-i-i-n-d you." I was the only one who laughed at this remark, because Ed and I were the only ones who had heard that eerie refrain in the graveyard back in Kentucky.

The next night, when the sea had returned to its normal bobbing, we were back in our spot on the deck next to the ropes. John had stopped by for his regular nightly visit. Tonight, instead of holding Fred in his lap, he did the opposite. He stretched out on the quilt and put his head in Fred's lap, using him for a pillow. His long legs stuck out onto the deck.

I asked him to tell us a bedtime story, so he told us the German version of *Rumpelstilzchen*. It was a lot like the story we were familiar with, but when he finished, I commented that the little man in the German account was meaner than the one we had been told in America.

John replied, "Bad guys in fairy tales are a lot like pirates. Some are kind of mean, but others are *very* mean."

I whirled around and looked at him. "Pirates? Why did you mention pirates?" I asked. "There's no way we could be in danger of pirates on the *Sunny Sloop*, is there?"

John patted me on the back, laughing. "Calm down, little *Fraulein*. It's not at all likely that we will encounter pirates on this passenger ship. We've been told, though, that since we are entering North America through New Orleans and are passing by islands where pirates are known to hide out, there is a slim chance they could make an appearance. That's why the captain called a meeting of all the men on the ship today, so we would have a plan of action in the unlikely event we might bump into any pirates."

John could tell by the look on my face that I was still worried about this thought, so he went on. "But look around you. Why would pirates want to try to steal anything off a ship like this?"

"Yeah, Emma Mae," Edward said. "And besides, if we *do* run into some pirates, me and John can always scare them off with our pocket knives." They both laughed, but I didn't feel amused.

John yawned and stretched his arms over his head. "Look," he said, "I'm sorry I mentioned it. It's really nothing to worry about.

Just go to sleep now. I know that's what I'm going to do." He yawned again. "*Gute Nacht*, my dear *Kinderlein*," he said as he turned to leave. "Be of good cheer."

It was somehow reassuring to hear John refer to us as his dear children.

"*Gute Nacht*, John." Edward and I said in unison as he walked away into the darkness. Fred was already asleep.

Now that John was gone, it seemed especially quiet in our space on the deck. Edward and I talked once again about what magical thing had happened that had brought us back in time. We went over the event again and again.

As we were both getting drowsy we could see the flashing of a thunderstorm out at sea. Suddenly, Edward sat up. With a note of excitement in his voice he said, "Emma Mae? Do you think it could have been the lightnin'? Was our change-over connected somehow to the thunderstorm?"

"Hmmmm," I said. "It was definitely storming when we left there, and a terrible storm was happening when we arrived here. You know, Ed, you might be onto something."

Edward lay back down and closed his eyes. "It's an interestin' thought, at least," he said drowsily.

"Yes," I agreed. "I'd rather think about that idea than to wonder what will become of us if we don't ever find a way to go back."

"I don't even want to think about it," he mumbled. He was almost instantly asleep, but I turned over and lay awake awhile . . . watching the thunderstorm as it flickered in the distance. I dared to let my thoughts wander again to the question of what our future would hold if we never discovered a way to get back home.

But as I twirled my necklace and drifted off to sleep, there was no way I could know that a lone figure had gone sneaking away from behind some large coils of ropes following our discussion. Nor could I know that the person was wearing a devious smile.

CHAPTER 17

I woke up the next morning feeling tired. There was still an uneasy feeling in the pit of my stomach. I knew that John was right—pirates were not something I needed to be overly concerned about. As we returned from eating our small servings of molasses-flavored mush and milk, I was reminded of another reason for my uneasiness. Tater.

Tater seemed to be near us everywhere we went. He was constantly making loud remarks to anybody around about being paying passengers. Just this morning he had commented on how small the servings of mush had been. Then he said loudly to the people around him, "If we didn't have all these extra mouths to feed, we'd all be a lot better off." As usual, he was looking directly at us when he said it.

To get my mind off Tater, I took the journal from my pocket. I needed to update the story about our time on the *Sunny Sloop*. So many things had happened, I didn't want to get behind in my writing.

About mid-morning John came for his daily visit. As we talked, I looked up to see Tater peeking out from behind one of the large coils of rope, partly hidden by a lifeboat. He was spying on us, as usual. I decided I needed to talk to John about it.

"What's the situation with Tater?" I asked quietly. "Why is he always looking at us with that mean look on his face?"

John turned around and spotted Tater behind the lifeboat.

"Who, Tater?" he asked loudly. Too loudly. I hadn't wanted Tater to know we were talking about him. "Why, Tater's just a chicken," he said. "He may look mean, but that's just the impression he wants to give. He's not brave enough to do anything even if he wanted to. Just a chicken," he repeated.

I glanced back in Tater's direction. His eyes were narrowed and the sneer had disappeared. It had been replaced by a determined-looking glare.

"Naw, no problem with Tater," John went on, still talking a notch or two louder than I would have liked. "I guess you could say he's not even a chicken. He's more like a fuzzy baby chick," John laughed.

I decided to change the subject somewhat. "Do you know where Tater got his nickname?" I asked. I glanced back toward the lifeboats. Tater was gone.

"Yes, his father was a potato farmer back in Germany," John began. "The story goes that Tater, whose real name is Henry, almost died when he was born. The only thing they could feed him was a thin broth of potato soup. That's what saved his life. After that, all he wanted to eat was potatoes. So that's where he got the name."

John gestured with one hand, smiling. In his other hand he held out a wooden piece that looked exactly like a small brown potato. He had been whittling while we were talking. He handed the piece to me.

"How do you *do* that?" Edward asked. He was still fascinated by John's whittling ability.

"Practice, my man, practice," John smiled, patting Edward on the back.

He stretched out his long legs and continued, "You know, since the famine has come to Germany, most potato farmers are having a hard time getting by. That's why Tater's family is moving to America, hoping to start over in the new land."

"I never heard you say for sure, but is that why your family is going to America, too?" Edward asked.

"Our family?" John responded. "No, we're not potato farmers, but, as you know, we are people of the earth. We raise fruits and vegetables for eating. I think my parents decided to move to America because they were ready for something new and different. They decided to pull up the family roots and transplant them somewhere new."

"How do you feel about their decision to move to a whole new land?"

"Well, the way I've been taught, you don't ask your elders why. You just trust that they make the best decisions. And once they decide something, there's no turning back. It's all part of the old German tradition, I guess you could say."

He stood up, stretched and yawned, and started to leave. As he walked away, he turned back and grinned. "By the way. Don't let any chickens get to you today," he teased. Then he was gone.

Edward looked at me. "I hope he's right," he said. "Surely Tater is just a chicken and not a hawk like the ones we see soarin' in the sky back home, lookin' for something to attack for food." With his whittling knife and a block of wood in his hands, he moved over and sat down near where Fred was playing in the coiled-up ropes.

We had discovered that the rats that lived in the ropes were not a problem, after all. They kept their distance, and, ever since that terrible nightmare, I kept mine.

But not our little Fred. Always the animal lover, he had actually made a pet out of one of the baby rats. He would hold a crumb of food in his hand and the rat would stand on its hind legs to eat it.

"Fred," I asked, "have you named your pet yet?"

"Sure," he answered. "His name is Clyde."

"Clyde?" I laughed. "Why Clyde?"

"Because Clyde's the biggest rat back at Sunny Slope School."

Edward and I laughingly agreed. "Just like Tater," I thought.

The day passed slowly. In mid-afternoon, Margareta and Elizabeth came to see us for a while. They squealed and acted horrified by Fred and his pet rat, but at least they were well entertained.

When they left, Fred tagged along with them to spend some time playing games in their quarters. He left Clyde behind in his home in the ropes.

They hadn't been gone long when I looked up to see the real Clyde look-alike approaching. He and George, the red-faced man with the bushy brown beard, were walking in our direction. George was the one who had caught the stowaway when we first arrived. He was also the one who had wanted to throw our great-grandfather's fruit cuttings overboard.

"Young lady," George began. "Tater, here, tells me you are traveling without your parents."

"Yes, sir, that's true," I said, smiling my most pleasant smile. "I think that is common knowledge."

"H-h-how long have your parents been in America?" he asked. He appeared to be very nervous.

"Long enough to buy property and build a small house for us to live in when we arrive," I answered.

Edward came to stand beside me as I faced Tater and George. He slipped his knife in his pocket and crossed his arms with a defiant look on his face.

George looked around nervously. He hesitated for a minute, shuffling his feet while his eyes darted from one of us to the other. I decided this was a good time to ask some questions of my own.

"Why do you ask, sir? As you can see, we are well-behaved German children who are as anxious to get to our new surroundings as anybody else." I smiled politely at the uneasy man in front of me.

"W-w-well," he began. He coughed softly and squirmed a bit uncomfortably before continuing. His usually red face was even redder.

"Well, you see, T-T-Tater, here," he gestured with his head, "told me that he is wondering whether or not you have proper papers and passports for making this journey on our ship. Heh, heh. I'm sure everything is in order, but Tater, here, has been trying to get me to ask about it for quite a few days now. Heh, heh. For instance, d-d-do you have papers that show you've paid for the food you're eating, use of the facilities, attending our school, and other expenses?"

I had known in advance that this topic would most likely come up. I had actually lain awake at night, planning what to say if it did.

Now I gave Tater a cold stare for a few long seconds before looking Mr. Bushy-Beard George straight in the eye. I took a step closer to him.

"If you'll excuse me, sir, may I first ask *you* a few questions? By what authority are you asking to see our papers? Are you acting as an official? Are you checking everybody's papers, or are you singling out three innocent children who are bravely traveling to meet their parents in a new country?"

My voice had gotten louder than I intended. It caught the attention of some of the other passengers who were sitting on the open deck, but by this time I was really feeling angry. With my hands on my hips, I moved even closer to him.

"While we're at it, Mister George, I have some *more* questions for you. If you're so interested in checking us out, why don't you ask the other passengers if they think we're creating a problem? Ask the cooks if we're causing a food shortage. Find out from the people around us if they have a complaint." I could tell that my face was getting red as I was talking in a raised, angry voice.

"Well, now, I didn't mean to get you upset," George said. "It's just that . . . that . . . well, you *are* the ones who stopped me from pitching those nasty twigs overboard one day." He pulled on his collar again. "And you *did* talk smart and turned everybody against me after that."

Tater jumped in. "Mister George, " he said, "these people are enjoying life as much as any people on this ship, and . . . and . . . and I know they haven't paid for *any* of it."

"If what you say is true," George stammered, "we . . . we need to start a list . . ."

I couldn't stand it any longer. I got right in his face and said, "If you're so concerned about all this, why don't you skip the list and go to the captain and tell *him* you think we might be traveling without proper papers and permissions and see how *he* responds?"

Even as those words left my lips, I knew it was possible the idea could backfire on me. George might truly go to the captain later—but, for the moment, the challenge seemed to work. He squirmed while tugging on his shirt collar.

"Don't get so upset, young lady, I . . . I . . . I wouldn't have mentioned any of these things, except . . ."

"I know!" I interrupted, moving even closer to him and staring him straight in the eye at close range. "I know! Tater, here, wanted you to!"

George mopped his head with his handkerchief. He shrugged his shoulders and nodded. Then he turned and walked rapidly away. He was so embarrassed his face seemed to be glowing.

But Tater, walking beside him, wouldn't let the matter die.

"Mr. George," we heard him say, "why *don't* we go to the captain? He can find out about all of this . . ." His voice grew fainter as the two of them walked on down the deck away from us.

Edward and I looked at each other as we sat back down on our quilt. "What do we do now?" Edward asked.

"I don't know, Ed. I'm afraid we haven't heard the end of it," I answered quietly. "Like I told you, Tater has been suspicious of us from the very beginning. Now it looks like the chicken is turning into a hawk, after all. I'm afraid he's finally out to get us."

CHAPTER 18

In mid-afternoon we heard the sounds of accordion music coming from the open courtyard of the ship. It was a windy day, with the sails billowing overhead. Since we had nothing else to do, we decided to walk over and see what was happening.

As usual, there was a large group of children clapping their hands in rhythm to the music. Adults, too, had crowded around the area. The girl in the red scarf was there with the man. This time as I looked at them I noticed a strong family resemblance. They had to be father and daughter. Neither of them smiled, but both of them looked nervously around the crowd.

I looked back at the performers who were playing German folk music. After watching for a minute, I glanced back at the red-scarf family . . . but the girl was no longer there.

"Ed," I whispered, "the girl has disappeared."

"I know," he answered. "I was watching her."

"Where do you think she's gone . . . and what do you think she's up to?"

"Good questions, and I aim to find out. Save my space. I'll be back."

And with that, he was gone. I looked around just in time to see him disappearing around the tall mast in the center of the ship. He was gone for what seemed an eternity. Just before the show ended, he was back at my side, wearing a worried look on his face.

"What happened?" I whispered. "Did you learn anything?"

Edward nodded his head gravely. "I'll tell you later."

At that moment, out of the corner of my eye, I saw movement. It was the girl returning. The man raised his eyebrows at her. She smiled at him and nodded her head, indicating that she had obviously achieved what she had been gone to do. The man returned her smile, then gave her a small hug, all the time looking around nervously.

I joined the crowd in applauding the accordion players for providing music for our entertainment. As we started to leave, though, I glanced back at the red scarf family just in time to see the father gazing at Edward and me with raised eyebrows. The look on his face seemed to be more than a look. It appeared to be a warning.

When we got back to our space, Fred was ready for a spin around the boat. I gave him permission and away he went.

"Tell me! Tell me! What happened?" I asked as we sat down.

"Well, I followed the girl from a distance," he said in a secretive-sounding voice. "I was careful to hang back so she wouldn't see me if she looked around. At first, she walked as though everything was normal. She crossed to the main part of the ship where the rich people have those little rooms.

"I peeped around the corner and watched. She used a key to open a door to one of the first-class berths. After she went inside, I snuck to the doorway to peep in, just as she was openin' a trunk. I couldn't see what she was takin', but she slipped something out of the trunk and put it into a small bag she was wearin' underneath her shirt. When she started closin' the trunk, I left and hurried back to the program on deck. I'm sure she didn't see me."

"Remind me to hire you if I ever need an investigator, Detective Edward. It sounds like you did a good job of spying. But I'm wondering something. Did you see the warning look her father gave us after she got back? It was enough to give me the shivers again."

Edward said, "Yes, I saw it. It might be because we were both looking at them. We'll have to be more careful about watching them so much."

"I'm sure you're right. Since he did stare at us with mean-looking eyes, though, I think we need to tell somebody. But who?"

"Why, our family, of course."

Just as we started to get up, Fred returned to our space, panting from his run around the ship. "You're just in time," I said. "We're going down below."

We hustled down the steps to the large room where our family was gathered in their little space. We quickly told them about the actions of the man and the girl.

"What do you think we should do?" I asked.

Johann said, "Since you don't know what it was the girl took, I think it's too early to share it with the ship's captain. Let's wait and see if the same thing happens again. If it does, we'll need to tell him what's going on. Surely he'll know how to handle the situation."

That night after supper, we spent time sharing games and stories with our family. Then the three of us climbed the ladder on our way to our private spot on deck.

When we got to the top of the steps, to our great surprise, the tall man with the red scarf was standing there with his arms crossed. He didn't say a word, but he didn't have to. His look said it all. After glaring at the three of us for a few seconds, he turned and walked away, disappearing into the shadows of the night.

I whispered, "I don't know about you fellows but that look gave me the heebie-jeebies."

"Me, too," Fred said, grabbing my hand.

"Not me," Edward said. "I'm going to find out what's goin' on." And with that, before I could say a word, Edward, too, disappeared into the darkness.

"Wait, Ed! You come back here," I called softly in my big sister voice. "Come back here!" I said again. "I mean it!" But he was gone.

"Come on, Freddie," I whispered, still holding his hand. "Let's get on to our own space. He'll surely be back soon."

I was right. We hadn't been on our pallet long when, out of the darkness, Edward appeared.

"That was too dangerous!" I said curtly. "You know you're in trouble when your big sister refuses to talk to you." I crossed my arms and turned my back to him.

"Wait a minute, Emma Mae," Edward replied. "Don't judge me until you hear my case." This was an expression we had heard Papa say to Mama on different occasions when they didn't see eye-to-eye about something.

For some reason that struck me as funny. I turned to face him, grinning. "All right, then. Since you made it back safely, go ahead and tell us what happened."

"It was so dark in that area of the ship, I didn't know for sure where he was. I'll admit it was pretty scary, walkin' around the stacks of cargo and those tall masts. I had no idea which way he had gone, so I crept around, hopin' to spot him without bumpin' into him."

"Did you?" I asked.

"Did I spot him or did I bump into him?" Edward laughed.

"You know what I mean. Did you spot him?"

"Yes. Once he got out on the open deck at the far end of the ship, there was enough light that I could barely see him. But you'll never believe where he disappeared."

"Tell us! Tell us!" Fred said.

"In the ship's hold."

"In the ship's *what*?" Fred asked.

"You know, Freddie, at the stern or back of the boat, there's a place where all kinds of things are stored—like boxes and trunks and stuff. It has an openin' that's not much bigger than a huge rat hole."

"So how did you see him go into such a small space?" I asked.

Edward answered, "By pure luck. He had no idea he was bein' followed. Just as I stuck my head around the back mast of the ship, I saw him disappear. He crawled into that little openin'."

"I've seen that space before," I said. "I don't see how a grown man can fit in there—much less share the space with his daughter."

"If him and that girl live in a place the size of a rat hole, then they must be kinda like people rats." Fred said sleepily.

"People rats. I like that description, little Fred," I said, smiling.

"We can walk to that area again tomorrow and check it out in daylight," Edward yawned. "Now, judgin' from my heavy eyelids, it's about time for me to get some shut-eye."

"Yes, it is time for us to say our prayers and go to sleep," I agreed, but Fred was already snoozing. In no time at all, Edward joined him.

For some reason, though, the usual gnawing of the rats in the ropes near my head made me feel uneasy tonight. Even a bit frightened. I tugged on my necklace as I finally drifted off to sleep.

CHAPTER 19

Another day dawned. It was hazy with a moderate breeze. We knew that today was washday. A portion of the quarterdeck was screened off with a spare sail set up like a screen. This created a bathing place for the women, girls, and small children. This was occasionally done early in the morning. Margareta came to get me so we could go together. I looked for the girl with the red headscarf, but she didn't show up.

Later in the morning the men and boys had their chance to wash. Edward and Fred went along with John. They had a great time, throwing buckets of water on each other.

It wasn't until after a lunch of hardtack and milk that we learned there was to be a birthday party on board the ship for all people who had September birthdays. Since Edward was one of those, we, naturally, went to the gathering. Most of the ship's passengers were out on this beautiful bright afternoon. A brisk wind blew us quickly across a choppy sea.

As usual, Fred went with Bessie to sit on the floor near the front.

He had barely left when Edward said, "Don't look now, but the rats have emerged from their hole."

I knew he meant the "red scarf family." I glanced to see that, as before, they stood at the back edge of the crowd.

John came walking up to where we stood, bouncing along in the way he always did when he walked. "*Guten Tag*," he said cheerfully. "Since I'm going to be one of the judges this afternoon, don't expect any assistance from me. Each person is on his or her own today." He winked at us, smiling.

"Don't you worry about doing us any favors, mister," Edward responded. "We'll be able to take care of ourselves without any help from the likes of you." We all laughed good-naturedly.

The games were to include a three-legged race, leap frog, and tug-of-war. When I saw that Edward was caught up in the competition of the games, I decided it was up to me to do the spying today, in case the girl disappeared.

I didn't have to wait long before I saw her slip away from the crowd. It was as though she just melted away. The man stood looking straight ahead, watching Edward's every move with a mean-looking scowl on his face. I knew at that point he wasn't watching me, so I, too, slinked away into the shadows of the ship.

I tried to remember what Edward had said about following the girl without being seen. Not being a detective like Ed, it was hard for me to do. I just knew she would come popping around a corner at any time and catch me.

As luck would have it, I got to the corner of the decking and peeked around—just in time to see her vanish around the next corner. Cautiously, I moved to that spot, stealing a look into the main walkway where the first-class berths were located. When I saw her stop in front of a door, I drew my head back, in case she looked to see if anyone was following her. After a terrifying minute had passed, I dared to look again. This time I saw her red scarf disappearing into the cabin.

I quickly acted out what Edward had said. I sneaked to the doorway and peeked inside. The girl was opening a trunk. That was all I needed to know. We had seen her in action twice now. Surely that would be enough evidence to prove that she was stealing from the passengers.

When I got back to the party, my heart was racing—I didn't know whether from fear or excitement. I just hoped I had not been missed during the games.

A short time later, when the competition ended, both Edward and Fred came racing up to where I stood. Both of them were out of breath from the tug-of-war. They were excited because their team had won the war, even without John's help.

Lines formed as a large cake was brought out and served to everybody present. I joined John and Margareta and the rest of our family in line, but out of the corner of my eye I saw the girl return. As before, she came to stand at her father's side. He gave her a quick hug before they slinked away from the crowd like a disappearing act.

Later, when I whispered what I had done, Edward was surprised. He patted me on the back, giving me one of his special smiles. "Way to go, Sis," he said quietly.

When it was suppertime, we went to eat in the 'tween deck with our family. I told them how I had followed the girl and watched her go into another berth while the party was going on.

Johann said, "It sounds as though these two people are stealing our passengers blind and they have no idea. They think their possessions are safely locked away in their own berths. I don't imagine they even check those things often since they are all under their own lock and key. I know I hardly ever check our trunk."

He rubbed his chin, just the way Papa does. "It's time for me to get an appointment with Captain Lott so we can share this story. I'm not sure how soon he will be able to see us, though. It may take a day or two before he will get us scheduled."

"That's all right, I said. "Just knowing that you'll help us do the right thing is what counts."

By the time we got back to our space on deck, it was not quite dark. The setting sun had just dropped into the sea, leaving a bright spot in the western sky.

"Why don't we take a stroll around the deck, boys?" I asked.

I looked at Edward and winked. "Sure thing, Sis," he answered, winking back. "We have time to stroll all the way around the deck before we go to bed."

Fred, always interested in running around the ship, said excitedly, "Bet I can beat both of you this time." Before he set off at a run, I cautioned him that he needed to run quietly because some of the people were already getting ready to sleep.

Edward and I walked nonchalantly to the bow of the ship. Fred, who had already taken a spin around the deck, caught up with us just as we got to the front. The cool stiff breeze almost took my breath away.

While we were there, I leaned out far enough so I could see the figurehead once again. I still thought the huge sun with a smile on its face and the words "SUNNY SLOOP" carved below it was unusual for a ship of this size.

After Edward and I had enjoyed the view for several quiet minutes, we turned and continued our evening stroll. The stars had begun to twinkle overhead. I told our exuberant Fred he could make one last run.

At the opposite end of the ship, we stopped to look at the frothy path in the ship's wake. Once again Fred ran up in time to look at the scene with us. For children from the countryside in western Kentucky, this sight was still unbelievable.

While we did, in fact, enjoy looking at this scene, I also remembered the real purpose for our coming to this area—and that was to take a silent, discreet look at the opening to the ship's hold where Edward had seen the man disappear last night.

We were turning slowly away from the rail when suddenly, from out of the blue, Fred asked, much too loudly, "Do you see any *rat holes* around here, Edward?"

Both Ed and I gasped, putting our fingers to our lips. There was one thing we *didn't* want to do, and that was to alert anybody lurking nearby that we were in their area.

Hurriedly, we started walking away from the rail, heading back toward our own place near the lifeboats, but not before I saw movement inside the dark space . . . and it was definitely *not* a rat.

CHAPTER 20

We were awakened the next morning by raindrops blowing into our small, protected space by the lifeboats. The ship bobbed up and down more than usual in the choppy sea. Crewmembers dashed all around, raising and lowering sails and tying down anything that wasn't attached. We folded our quilts and stashed them in our dry nook, then took off at a run to join our family in their place between the decks.

After breakfast, we gathered in the familiar space that was beginning to feel like home. Johann told us he had just received word that the captain would allow us a brief visit this morning.

So it was that Johann, John, Edward, and I made our way to the main deck. The wind was much more blustery by now, with the rain pelting down. We dashed across the open space to the captain's quarters with my heart flapping as fast as the wind-filled sails.

Johann rapped on the door. "It's not locked," Captain Lott called sharply. "Come on in."

We hurried inside, out of the rain. In the dim light given off by swaying lanterns, I quickly scanned the inside of the cabin. It was a small plain room with a single bed, a wardrobe, and a chest. In the center of the room there was a table and four chairs. He indicated that we should sit.

As the three men took their seats at the table, Edward offered me the fourth chair. He stood quietly behind me.

The captain glanced at us with a worried look. "And what business is so important that it had to be brought to my cabin this stormy morning?" he asked in a gruff voice.

"We apologize for the urgency, sir, but these children have made some observations we feel you should know about," Johann answered. He then proceeded to tell the captain what we had seen.

"Hmmm," Captain Lott said, stroking his chin. A furrow still puckered his forehead, but the glare had left his eyes. "I know the family you're speaking of. They appeared on board our ship at the last minute, just as we set sail from Bremen."

His harsh gaze focused first on me and then on Edward but, as his eyes searched our faces, his look softened. "So not only are you being accused of traveling without proper papers, which is what I have been told, but you are also trying to convince me that someone is stealing from my passengers."

He stood and began pacing back and forth with his hand stuck inside the front of his jacket. "I don't see how we can confront them without more evidence than being spied on by children."

John spoke up quickly. "If you'll excuse me, sir, my father and I can vouch for the integrity of these children. I have no doubt but what they say is true."

"I agree," Johann said in his deep voice. "They have no reason to conceive a story that is not real."

"I understand," said Captain Lott, waving his hand, "but still, I think we'll have to catch them 'red handed,' as they say, and find out where they are putting these treasures you tell me they are taking."

I decided to join the conversation. "Sir, if you will allow me, I have a suggestion to make."

The captain stopped his pacing and looked at me again with that deep, dark stare. "And just what is that?"

"My brother and I have noticed that the girl always sneaks away from the crowd when there's a program taking place and most of the passengers are on deck. Why don't we wait until Sunday when there will be a worship service? That is usually attended by most of the ship's passengers."

"Yes, yes," he said. His face softened again, and his eyes met mine. "Go on with your train of thought."

"What if you had some of your officers follow the girl and see where she goes and what she does? That way you will be able to get to the bottom of this."

"Hmmm," he said. "Good suggestion, young lady. And in the meantime, my officers can try to find out exactly where the man and his daughter stay at night. No doubt, that will be the place where the stolen items are kept, if, in fact, there are stolen items."

He paused for a long moment, looking directly at Edward and me, saying, "If this turns out to be a wild goose chase, you children are the ones who will be punished instead of them."

We nodded our heads. "We understand, sir. Thank you for hearing our story," I said as I dropped into a small curtsy.

"Yes, *danke*, sir," Edward added, bowing, before we hurried toward the door. I looked back to see the captain with a soft smile on his face as he watched us go.

The four of us dashed through the rain, back to the space 'tween decks where our family was sitting out this day on a wind-tossed sea.

Later in the evening, following our meal of salted beef and mushy potatoes, Edward went up on deck and found out that the rain had finally stopped. We told our family good night and went to our own private space. Since our quilts were still dry, we spread them out to make our bed.

The ship continued to lurch for a bit, causing my stomach to lurch with it. It wasn't long, though, until the swaying slowed and the sea became calm.

Now the clouds rolled away, leaving a clear night sky. The stars looked so close I felt as though I could reach up and touch them. But the most unusual thing happened. Even though there was no storm, flashes of silent lightning continued to flare all around. I fell asleep hoping that wasn't a bad omen.

CHAPTER 21

The clanging of a bell the next morning was the signal that this was a school day. Both Margareta and I had been selected to be helpers, assisting the younger students with their lessons while the teacher worked with others. The time passed quickly.

When our school session ended, the teacher announced there was to be a foot race for anyone who wanted to participate. Each person had to run around the deck five times.

Both Edward and Fred took part. When they finished the race, they both flopped down on our quilt. Edward was acting out of sorts because young Frederick had won the race, even beating his big brother.

Apologetically, Fred said, "It's because I practice so much, Edward. And I've always been a good runner, even back home."

Edward glared at Fred for a minute, but then he grinned. "It's all right, Freddie. I was just teasing. Don't fret about it. I'm actually proud of you." He reached over and ruffled Fred's hair. "But you'd better watch out next time," he added. "I'll beat your socks off!"

After the boys had rested a bit, we sat on our quilt passing the time by playing "One Potato, Two Potato"—a favorite family game. We looked up to see Tater and George approaching again, but this time there were three in the group. They had dared to bring the captain with them. We jumped up as they approached.

"All right, all right," Captain "Jiggs" barked at George. "This had better be important for you to drag me down here in the middle of the day to see children."

"W-well, s-sir," George began. His usual red face was redder than ever. He had begun to perspire. "It seems that T-Tater, here, has reason to believe that this group of children are on board our ship without permission."

"So. What harm are they doing?" the captain asked sharply. "What kinds of problems have they created?" He glanced quickly at each one of us. His eyes smiled a little when he saw Fred stroking his pet rat.

He turned and looked directly at Tater and George. They pulled away from him as he turned his stare on them.

Tater didn't say a word. He only stood there, looking uncomfortable, shuffling his feet. But since George had gone this far, he had to state his case.

"W-well, s-sir" he began again, "according to T-Tater, here, they just kind of showed up one day, in the middle of a thunderstorm. Since that time he has overheard them talking about not being paying passengers, and, in the meantime, they have been eating our food, taking up space, using the ship's facilities, attending our school. Things like that."

Sweat was trickling down George's face now. He reached in his pocket and pulled out a soiled handkerchief to wipe it off. He was talking very fast. He knew he had to because the captain was looking at him sternly, crossing his arms and drumming his fingers on his elbows.

"Tater, here, says the little one over there even got sick and used the services of the ship's doctor and the minister."

The captain looked kindly at Fred for a brief moment, sitting there with his cute, snaggle-toothed grin, holding his rat. "So you're one of our survivors, are you?" He shook his head and closed his eyes.

Then he looked sternly at George and Tater. "I don't know why a matter of such small significance has been brought to my attention," he said emphatically. "These children don't look as if they would so much as harm a hair on a rat's head." George hung his head in an embarrassed way, but Tater stared straight at the captain.

"I have to go now," Captain Lott said as he turned to leave. He stopped and looked at us again. "I was about to say something. What was it? Oh, yes. Now I remember. If it should turn out that you are indeed non-paying passengers, we'll deal with the matter in an appropriate way, if *these people* insist." He rolled his eyes in the direction of Tater and George. "We'll talk about it again tomorrow." He looked back around at us. "You will, of course, have a chance to speak on your own behalf at that time."

Before he turned away, he winked at Edward and me and patted Fred on the head. He stuck his hand inside the front of his jacket as he stomped away.

We looked at our accusers. Sweat was running down the sides of George's red face. He wiped it with his handkerchief. "Well, now, children. You heard what the captain said. We'll talk again tomorrow."

He turned and hurried away, practically running in his haste to get away from the scene. This left only Tater, who stood there with his arms crossed, smiling his hateful smile. His face was redder than usual, making the bumps look even larger.

Tater said, "This 'chicken's' not through with you yet. I *heard* you talking about this the first day I saw you. I was hiding in the shadows. Besides that, one night I even heard you talking about the strange way you got here. I *know* you're here without papers. Like the man said, we'll talk again . . . tomorrow!"

Then he stood up straight and tall, tilted his head back so that his sharp chin stuck out, and puffed out his chest. He put one foot directly behind the other and slowly turned himself around, looking exactly like Clyde!

Edward, with his fists doubled up, was really angry. I knew he was about to jump on Tater the same way he had lit into Clyde back on the Sunny Slope school grounds a few weeks ago, when the funniest thing happened!

Just as Tater turned around, Fred let his pet rat go. The rat scampered off to his home in the ropes. It just so happened that it ran right under Tater's feet. Tater jumped so high and yelled so loud, we thought at first he had been hurt. But instead, he took off running as fast as he could go. We couldn't tell which ran faster—Tater or the rat named Clyde! Tater never even looked back!

We doubled over in laughter. After the suspense of the last few minutes, we were glad to have something to laugh about.

For the moment, at least.

CHAPTER 22

On the following morning the sea was unruffled, with only a slight wind. The sails flapped idly against the masts. It was Sunday. People gathered as usual on the quarterdeck for a service of music, preaching, and prayers. As we approached, we heard violin music.

We took our usual place on the floor at the outer edge of the gathering. Before we got settled, we saw them at the rear of the assembly—the man with the scarf around his neck and the girl with the scarf on her head.

In looking around further, we also saw the pleasant-looking man who was second in command to the captain. I knew he was referred to as the quartermaster. He had always been friendly around us, especially smiling at Fred anytime we met him on the ship. Today he stood at the back of the gathering. He looked in our direction and winked.

On the other side, closer to the first class berths, stood another man who had befriended us from time to time. This man was called the first mate. He, too, looked at us out of the corner of his eye and nodded.

After the violin had played for a bit, the person who was the director of music on the ship had the people stand to sing. Just as we stood up, I saw a slight movement. It was the girl quietly slinking away. As she stepped back, so did the quartermaster and the first mate. They moved stealthily, not attracting attention. But what the two men didn't know was that our Detective Edward also snuck away into the background.

Reverend Paetznick, the ship's minister, was long-winded today. I was so nervous I couldn't keep my mind on a thing he said. When he finally finished his sermon, we stood for the final song. This was the time when the girl usually returned to her father's side.

Today, though, she didn't reappear. The man in the red neck scarf kept looking back—first over his left shoulder and then over his right. He looked very concerned. Just before the song ended, the quartermaster came to stand beside him. They talked together briefly before the two of them left together, with the quartermaster holding the man's arm in a tight grip. It was all done so quickly and quietly, nobody else seemed to notice.

Since we were sitting with Margareta and Bessie, I asked, "Do you mind if Fred stays with you for a few minutes? There's something I need to check on."

"Sure," Margareta answered. "He can go with us to get lunch."

"Perfect," I said. "I'll join you soon."

I turned and dashed in the direction the two men had gone, hoping to keep them in view so I could see what was going on. I peeped around the first corner I came to. There was nobody in sight. But when I hurried around the second corner, I nearly bumped into the group that was gathered there.

The ship's first mate was holding the struggling girl in a tight grip while he tried to tie ropes around her wrists. Edward was helping him with the ropes. The quartermaster stood close by, still clutching the arm of the man with the red scarf.

I stopped abruptly, looking to see if there was anything I could do. Suddenly, the man in the red scarf lunged away from the quartermaster. He reached inside his shirt and pulled out a large knife. As he did this, he grabbed me, pulling me close to him. He turned me so that his arm was across my chest. Then he held the knife in front of me. I was so scared, I couldn't even scream.

The man said, "Let me daughter go or this sassy little miss will be food for the fishes."

The two officers were caught totally off guard. It was obvious they didn't know what to do. Since it appeared my life was in danger, I stood there, helpless, pleading with my eyes for somebody to do *some*thing.

Finally the quartermaster found his voice. "Come now," he said. "Let's not do anything rash. We can surely talk about this peacefully."

"When I see ye tying me girl up with ropes, it leaves no room for talk. Let her go so we can get on with our plan for leaving the ship."

The first mate said, "Do I need to remind you, sir, that we're in the middle of the Atlantic Ocean? It's not possible for you to leave the ship, with or without your daughter."

The man replied, "I know more about these things than you. We're in the area of the ocean where there are inhabited islands. We plan to take the fortune we've collected here on the ship and live the rest of our lives in riches. And there's nothing you can do to stop us."

The girl started moving, struggling to get loose. The first mate still held her firmly by her shoulders. Edward, standing beside them, grabbed the ends of the ropes as she twisted and pulled. She suddenly turned toward Edward and kicked him hard on the leg. He let out a yell as he grabbed his leg. When he did this, the ropes slipped out of his hands.

The first mate, though, was as slick as the girl. He reached around her, putting a hold on her much like her father had on me. The big difference was—the father had a knife pointed toward my heart and the first mate was unarmed.

The father spoke again. "I'll tell you one more time. I mean business! Let me Priscilla go before I hurt this lass. I happen to know we're coming close to the island we mean to call our home. We've got a lifeboat on the other side of the galley that's loaded with everything we need. All we have to do is add the treasures we've been collecting and we'll be ready to launch."

He rolled his eyes from side to side, looking wildly at the two officers. "Me and me girl are going to that island where we'll start our new life. So what happens to this snoopy miss? She be going with us when we leave the ship, alive . . . or dead. That all depends on you." As he said these last words, he moved the knife even closer to my pounding heart.

My mind was working fast. How was I going to be able to slip out of the strong grip this man had on me?

Suddenly, Priscilla jerked free from the first mate's hold. She raised her foot and kicked him in the stomach, causing him to double over in pain. The father tightened his grip around me. He said, "Come, Priscilla. Get behind me and be ready to move. If they don't do what I say, I might have to hurt the girl."

Just as he made that remark, the most unexpected thing happened. A small boy popped around the corner of the hallway and shouted loudly, "What's going on here?"

Priscilla's father whirled around to see who had yelled those words—and that was just what the officers needed. They immediately sprang into action. The quartermaster knocked the knife out of the father's hand and punched him backward, freeing me to get out of the way.

While that was happening, the first mate seized Priscilla again and held her tightly.

I ran to Fred and grabbed him in my arms. Edward was immediately at our side.

The father was still staggering from the unexpected blow. The quartermaster grabbed him again, this time turning him so that his hands were twisted behind his back. Then he pulled a whistle from his pocket and began to blow it, loud and shrill.

In no time, sailors swarmed in from all directions. When they saw the captives, they let out a cheer. They had all been suspicious of the two from the time they set foot on deck, but had no way of knowing what they were up to.

When Captain Lott appeared a few minutes later, he smiled at the three of us standing off to the side. Then he looked at Priscilla and her father with their hands tied behind them.

"So we caught the thieves red-handed, did we? I never had a doubt but what you would catch them," he said, looking at us. "We'll take them down to the lowest deck with the livestock. They can join the two stowaways down there until we get to land."

As crewmembers took the pair away to their on-ship prison, the captain looked at the two chief officers who had been involved and asked, "Now, where *is* all this treasure I've been hearing about? We'll need to restore all of it to the rightful owners."

The quartermaster looked at the first mate. The first mate looked at the quartermaster. They both had blank looks on their faces. They shrugged their shoulders.

"Don't worry about that," Edward said. "We know exactly where the treasures are."

Fred added, "You know rats live in holes, don't you? We can show you the hole where these rats lived."

"We feel sure that's where you'll find the stolen items," I added.

And with that, three children from Kentucky, on board the *Sunny Sloop* with their ancestors who were headed for America, led the procession of officers to the hold in the back of the ship where all the passengers' treasures had been hidden.

We then checked out the area where the lifeboats were located. One of them had, in fact, been supplied with food and other items necessary for survival. It was ready to be lowered to sea level. All it lacked was the treasures and the two passengers.

Now that the adventure had ended, we were free to go between the decks to see our family and to share the unbelievable story.

After hearing our tale, John asked, "Does anybody know how they had gotten a key that would unlock all the cabins?"

Edward nodded. "I heard the captain telling about it. After we met with him, he found out that the man is a locksmith. He knows all about locks. He had special keys that could unlock any door or trunk on the ship. After he was caught, the man confessed that he's wanted in England for working as a burglar. He and his daughter had escaped to Germany a short time ago. They managed to slip away from the authorities back in Bremen just before the ship sailed."

"Nobody knows how they happened to get on board this ship," I added. "The captain was quite disturbed that a crook like that had managed to slip aboard, especially since there were two of them."

"How glad all of us are that you were able to help bring this case to justice," Johann said. "If you hadn't been so observant, the pair might have gotten away with all those families' treasures."

"In a way, they were kind of like on-ship pirates," John said, looking at me and winking.

Mary Katherine came over and gave each of us a hug. "Every person on this ship will be singing your praise for what you've done." We returned her hugs, smiling.

By now it was time for supper. After we ate, we were ready to go back to our quarters.

John embraced each of us before we left, saying gently, "*Gute Nacht, my Kinderlein. Sei guten Mutes.*"

We climbed back up the ladder to our on-deck home, relieved that this experience was behind us and that we were safe. But before I went to sleep, I tossed and turned again.

Two things kept bouncing around inside my head. One, in spite of all that had happened today, I knew there was one young man on the ship, by the name of Tater, who would definitely *not* be singing our praise . . . and, two, John had made another reference to pirates that brought chill bumps back to my arms and worry into my heart.

CHAPTER 23

It was just before dawn the next morning when I awoke with a start. Something didn't seem right. I looked around in the near-darkness. Both boys were snoozing quietly. Since the weather had been pleasant last night, other people were sleeping up on deck. Everything appeared to be normal—and yet I had a strong feeling that something was wrong.

I got up and walked to the railing. A pale hint of light in the east signaled the coming of day. The waters were calm, splashing gently against the sides of the ship. The tall sails billowed quietly in the breeze. I stood for several minutes, chiding myself for over-reacting to a feeling.

As I turned to go back to my sleeping space, I glanced again toward the brightening sky. This time, to my surprise, I saw the distant silhouette of another ship. While I had seen other ships in the distance before, this time it felt different.

Was it my imagination, or did the ship seem to be growing larger, even as I watched? If so, that meant it was moving a lot faster than we were. My feeling of foreboding was stronger than ever. A ship coming toward us from out of the near-darkness could not be a good sign. But, I reminded myself, there is nothing to worry about. John had said so.

I watched a minute longer, listening carefully to see if anyone else might have noticed the ship. Only the usual sounds of people sleeping and the lapping of water on the sides of the boat could be heard.

When I glanced back to see the other ship again, though still at a great distance, it definitely seemed to have grown in size. Inside my chest I felt a heavy sense of danger. It was so strong I couldn't ignore it.

Quickly, I went to where my brothers were sleeping and shook them awake. I pulled them to the railing where the three of us huddled, peering out into the dim light as the image of the other boat continued to grow larger, even as we watched. We wondered what we should do to alert the sleeping ship.

"Ed, go wake John and Johann. They'll know what to do,"

Edward immediately ran out of sight, moving through the now-familiar passageways and down the ladder to awaken our family.

The feeling of fear was tight in my chest as I watched the ship draw closer. It seemed to squeeze my heart. I hugged Fred tightly, wanting to protect him from the danger I felt certain was coming.

"Emma Mae," Fred said quietly. "Why do you think the lookout person up in the crow's nest is not waking everybody up?"

"That's it!" I exclaimed. "He must have fallen asleep up there. We need to wake him up so he can warn everybody. But how?"

"I can do it," he said bravely. Then, before I knew what was happening, he was out of the circle of my arms, running across the deck. I watched in horror as he started climbing up the rope ladder to the crow's nest.

"Freddie," I called loudly. "Frederick! Come back here! I mean it! Don't you climb up there! Wait! Let somebody else do it."

I was yelling this as I ran across the space where he had just gone. Behind me I heard voices calling: "Emma Mae? Fred? Where are you?"

It was Edward, returning with sleepy-looking John and Johann in tow.

Quickly I got their attention. "Look yonder," I yelled, pointing to the swinging ladder where a small figure was almost to the platform of the crow's nest. All around us people were waking up, grumbling, wondering what all the ruckus was about.

I looked across the water. In first light, I could see the ship drawing nearer by the minute.

We ran across the ship to the raised deck where the rope ladder was located. Just as we arrived, there was a yell from atop the platform. "Ship ahoy! Ship ahoy!" called the lookout from above. Then a horn blared, over and over, giving warning of possible danger to all those below.

Right away the ship's crew appeared from everywhere—sailors pulling on their britches, stuffing in their shirts, wiping sleep from their eyes. From across the way I saw that the captain had arrived, barking orders here and there, adding more confusion, since he didn't know what was going on.

I glanced back at the other ship as it skimmed across the water in our direction. It was smaller than the *Sunny Sloop*, which allowed it to move at a greater speed. I could barely make out the name of the ship that was printed near the bow. The ship's name was *Fortune Seeker*. As I watched, wondering whether or not it might truly be a pirate ship, there was a flash of fire, a puff of smoke, and a loud boom. A large splash of water erupted very near the side of the *Sunny Sloop* where I was standing.

Then another boom sounded—and another. Why, they were firing cannon at our unprotected ship! Each of the cannon balls landed closer than the one before. My heart was in my mouth!

Again, I looked at the crow's nest where my little brother had disappeared. It occurred to me that he might be safer there than he would be down below. When I looked back at the other ship, I saw that it was slowing down to come alongside. It was at that moment that I saw the flags!

At the top of their flagstaff, flying fully unfurled, was a flag that I recognized as being a Union Jack from England. But just below it, also flapping in the wind, was a black flag with a skull and crossbones. I recognized what it was just as the cry went up from all around: "*Piraten!* Pirates!"

Now that the captain knew what he was facing, he gathered all the men, both sailors and passengers, into a group at mid-ship and barked commands.

"You know what our plan is, so you know what to do," he shouted. "Hurry to your stations and prepare for action. But remember! We are a passenger ship! We have no cannon or guns, so we cannot combat the invaders in battle. That's an order! Now go!"

Immediately, the male passengers and crewmembers split into groups, some running forward toward the bow of the ship, some going aft toward the stern, while others hustled down the stairs 'tween decks. Many of the men remained in the middle of the ship near the captain. This included John and Johann. They were standing near the mainmast. Edward and I crouched behind them.

The pirates had lowered some of their sails by now, to match their speed with ours. As their ship eased ever closer, I noticed that many of our women and children had crowded inside the main cabin, the one where they had huddled for safety from the storm the day we arrived.

By now the two ships were so close together I was sure they would collide, but the pirates knew just what to do. While they were still a few yards off our ship's starboard side, the two vessels were close enough that several of the attackers came swinging across on ropes to board the *Sunny Sloop*. Quickly, they took other ropes and lashed the railings of the two ships together so that they were bound as one. When I saw knives and swords in their hands and guns stuck into the belts around their waists, I nearly fainted with fear.

Captain Lott stood on the elevated quarterdeck where he could see what was happening. I nearly jumped out of my skin when he bellowed: "We are not armed. There is nothing of value on board our passenger ship for you to take." Of course, he was yelling this in German.

Surprisingly, the pirate captain shouted his response in English. It was obvious he had understood at least part of the German message, though, because his response was, "Aye! That's whut they all say, me friend! But we won't take yer word fer it. Every ship has booty of some kind and we'll find yers . . . OR WE'LL KILL ALL THE PASSENGERS ON BOARD YER SHIP TRYIN'!"

It was obvious from the reactions that no one on board the *Sunny Sloop* had understood this message spoken in English. No one, that is, except Edward and me—and little Fred, who was high up in the crow's nest. We, like the pirate captain, had the advantage of understanding both languages.

Without speaking a word, Edward and I looked at each other. The thought flashed through my mind—if we let it be known we could understand English, we would be revealing our secret about our status on board the ship. But even with that fleeting thought, I did not hesitate. Neither did Edward. We had to do it.

Quickly, we told John and Johann what the pirate captain had just shouted. Their eyes reflected our own alarm. "You need to translate the messages for Captain Lott," John said. "Go! Hurry!"

"Right!" Edward and I said in unison. As we dashed toward the quarterdeck, I was so scared I thought my heart would thump right out of my body.

Before we could get to him, Captain Lott bellowed another message in German, "We cannot understand your words, but I'll tell you again. We are a passenger ship, only carrying families who are going to America. We have no treasures. Go away and leave us in peace."

Still speaking in English, the pirate captain roared, "Hah, hah, hah! No treasures, ye say? What about the fortunes of each family on board yer ship? What did they do? Leave all their riches behind in their homeland?"

This time his response brought laughter and hooting from the pirates. By now, other pirates had jumped over the railings that held our two ships together. They swished their swords through the air, letting our captain and crew know they were prepared to fight.

As I dashed toward the place where our captain stood, I heard a yell behind me. I whirled around to see a huge pirate with a wooden leg grabbing one of our young sailors and holding a knife at his throat. Even though the others seemed to be waiting patiently for the exchange of words between the ships' captains, they kept their swords and guns drawn. We knew they meant business.

Just before we jumped up onto the quarterdeck, Edward suddenly dropped to his hands and knees. I looked around to see that one of the pirates had spotted him. My heart leapt to my mouth when I saw the dirty-looking man in tattered clothes pull his knife from his belt. He grabbed Edward's hair and jerked him to his feet.

"And jest whar do ye think ye're a'goin', me boy?" he snarled as he held a knife to Edward's throat. His ugly, yellow teeth gleamed in the sunlight. Edward played dumb. He just shook his head and shrugged his shoulders, with his hands held out in front of him. His eyes were filled with fright.

"So ye don't speak English neither, do ye?"

Again Edward shook his head. He had a bewildered look on his face, as though he had no idea what the pirate was saying.

"Aw, ye're jest a scrawny little brat. Go ahead with your sneakin' around. A little runt like you cain't do nothing to hurt the likes o' us." And with that he roughly shoved Edward aside. Ed was still wearing that blank look on his face.

As soon as the pirate swaggered away, we leapt onto the platform with Captain Lott. In spite of the danger we were in, I couldn't help but smile a little when I saw the captain up close. He was wearing his usual black jacket, but beneath it, the tail of his nightshirt was hanging out. His hairy legs and bare feet stuck out below his clothing.

"*Kapitan! Kapitan!* Edward cried. "We have an urgent message for you." The captain jerked his head around and looked at us.

"What's this? What's this?" he muttered.

"We can translate what the pirates are saying," I said, speaking in German, of course.

"What's that? What's that?" he muttered.

He leaned closer to us and squinted his eyes in the dim early-morning light. "Why, you're the illegal passengers who helped catch the thieves!"

Edward said, "Yes, sir, but if you will let us, my sister and I can tell you exactly what the pirate captain is sayin' because we can speak his language."

The captain looked at each of us with a startled look on his face. "Are you saying that you can understand his language?"

"That's right, Captain Lott. We can understand everything he says." And with that I told him exactly what the pirate captain had just shouted.

Just as I finished the translation, the pirate leader bellowed again. "Halloo over there! Yer time is almost up! We need to know yer intentions afore the rest of us come aboard yer bloody ship and claim our treasures. If you decide to defend yerselves, **blood will be shed**! Ye've got one minute."

Edward translated this message for Captain Lott.

The pirates had obviously robbed passenger ships before. They knew we were basically defenseless. I felt sure that was why they were waiting so patiently for a response instead of storming the ship as soon as they came alongside, killing and looting like I thought pirates always did.

Just then John came running up. "Captain Lott," he yelled. "Everybody's ready! Edward, you come with me so we can know what they're saying. Emma Mae, you stay here and translate for the captain. It's time for action."

"*Ja! Ja!* Time for action," Captain Lott said, repeating John's words. But before he gave the signal for our men to take action, the pirate captain shouted again.

"If ye want to avoid bloodshed, run a white flag of surrender up yer flag pole! And be quick about it!"

The way the pirates allowed our people to move about was definitely a sign they were not feeling threatened by a ship full of unarmed men, women, and children.

The sun was well on its way up the sky by now. I looked at the crow's nest and could make out two people in the little space perched at the top of the tall mast. Fred will be safe up there when fighting breaks out, I thought.

The pirate captain yelled again. "Ahoy, over there! We see no flag, so we're comin' aboard!"

I told the captain what he said. Somewhere midway down the ship I heard Edward interpreting the message for the people near him.

John yelled from the large area below the main deck. "We're ready any time, sir. Let them come."

So now it was up to the captain.

"They need a response," he said, looking at me. "What shall I say? What shall I say?"

"Tell him the truth, sir," I suggested. "Tell him that we will not defend ourselves using guns or blades."

"*Ja. Ja,*" the captain said, nodding. He shouted exactly what I had told him to say.

"And tell him you hope God will have mercy on their souls for robbing and killing innocent children and their parents who are looking for a better way of life in a new country."

Once again Captain Lott called out my exact words.

I looked at the captain and said, "One more message, captain. Tell them that we give them permission to come aboard our ship in peace and take what they find here."

Captain Lott yelled my message. He did it with fervor, though, and sounded proud as he made the proclamation.

Then on his own, in his usual German language, he added, "*So sei es!!*"

The pirate captain responded with the same three little words, spoken in clear English: "So be it!"

CHAPTER 24

The next few minutes saw me cringing in the middle of another nightmare, except this one was real. As the pirates stormed aboard the *Sunny Sloop*, they yelled curses. Their knives and swords blazed in the sunlight. Many of them carried guns.

In spite of the noise and confusion, our own men stood still with their arms at their sides while more of the pirates came storming to the middle of the ship near the quarterdeck. As they charged closer, I saw that much of their clothing was dirty and ragged. Even from a distance, they smelled!

Our sailors had been told not to fight, but some of our younger ones drew their swords anyway. They joined in with the yelling and screaming that spread across the ship. The clashing of metal was all around me.

One of our sailors fell to the deck at midship. Blood spread across his shoulder where he had been struck by a blade. Another sailor took off, chasing the pirate who had injured our man. A sword fight followed between the two of them as blades slashed the air, clanging together when they struck. Our sailor stabbed the pirate's leg. He yelled loudly as he fell to the deck, holding his leg as blood spurted.

Gunshots rang out when still other pirates chased the sailor with the sword. I ducked and covered my head since they were close to where we stood.

I peeped between my fingers. Everywhere I looked in this nightmarish scene, I saw shiny swords and knives reflecting the sun's rays. Suddenly, a picture popped in my head about another nightmare where rats had glowing eyes. Today, even in the daylight, the eyes of the pirates seemed to be gleaming like rat eyes in this horrifying scene before me.

Some of the pirates rushed through the passageways to the sleeping and storage quarters on the main deck, knocking over everything and anybody standing in their way. I covered my ears so the shouts of the pirates and their terrible language would not be so loud.

A shot rang out nearby. One of our young sailors, trying to stop the pirates from entering the captain's quarters, grabbed his arm. Blood spread across his sleeve as they roughly shoved him out of their way. The ruffians stomped into the room, knocking over furniture and smashing cabinet doors in their search for treasures.

Others with guns and swords went storming down the 'tween decks area, yelling ugly words in English. I feared for our family and others who I knew must be huddled together in their little spaces.

One of them, his drawn knife glinting in the sunlight, charged into the cabin where some women and children were gathered with fear-filled faces. I cringed when I heard their screams of fright. It was terrifying. While the door to the cabin was open, though, I saw Tater, crouched safely in the middle of the group.

During all this action, I was partly hidden behind a beam on the quarterdeck beside Captain Lott. I covered my face with my hands, trying to blot out the horrible scene that was taking place before me. He stood with his arm around my shivering shoulders in a protective, fatherly way. I could feel him shaking, too. I was sure this was the first time he had ever encountered an invasion like this.

The captain and I both knew what the *Sunny Sloop's* basic plan was, but I had not been told what the signal would be for it to begin.

I was completely surprised when, just as one of our sailors slashed at a pirate, knocking him overboard into the sea, I heard a child's voice from up in the crow's nest shout: *"Bereit, fertig, los!"* Then in English he yelled, "Ready, set, go!"

At that signal, nets suddenly appeared. From all around the ship, fish netting of all sizes was quickly flung over the unsuspecting pirates. Immediately, our men tightened the nets and tied ropes around them, binding their entire bodies so that they could no longer fight. The pirates on board the *Sunny Sloop* were now our captives. From the time they had stormed across the railing onto our ship, the entire battle had only lasted a few minutes.

When the captain of the *Fortune Seeker* realized his band of pirates had been both tricked and captured, he let out a yell. "Man the cannons! We'll shoot their bloody boat outta the water!"

But it was no use. The few men who had remained on board his ship were being chased, captured, and tied up by Johann and some of our own sailors who had jumped over the railing during the fracas. Even the pirate captain was overpowered when a net was thrown over his head. He was bound with ropes like all the others.

John rushed to the captain on the quarterdeck. "The victory is ours!" he shouted in German. "The *Sunny Sloop* and her people are safe! Thanks be to God!"

This announcement was met with shouts of praise from the German immigrants and crewmembers that were spread across both ships.

As the shouting died down, I was surprised to hear Edward's voice echoing the same words, but shouting them in English. "The victory is ours! The *Sunny Sloop* and her people are safe! Thanks be to God!"

This time the announcement was met with moans and curses as the English-speaking pirates realized they had been both tricked and defeated.

The Graveyard

The struggling pirates on board our ship, tightly bound with nets and ropes, were led back onto the *Fortune Seeker*, kicking and swearing as they went. The *Sunny Sloop* crewmembers went from one pirate to another, removing the nets that had been flung over their heads, but making sure that their wrists and ankles remained securely tied. Then, to the pirates' great horror, every gun, sword, and knife was tossed overboard into the sea.

Captain Lott marched around the pirates' ship, barking out his orders. "No," I heard him shout, "we will *not* take food off their ship, even though we could use it. And, no, we will *not* touch their treasure chests full of booty. It is dirty plunder, taken by wicked people, and it does not belong to us. Therefore, we'll leave it where it is. May God have mercy on the souls of people who steal from others."

When Captain Lott made his next announcement, we were all surprised. He shouted: "Not only are we throwing the pirates' guns and swords away, but we are also heaving their cannonballs into the sea. If the children on the *Sunny Sloop* want to take part in this, let them come aboard the pirate ship and give the cannonballs a shove."

The German children squealed with delight when they were actually allowed to jump on board a real pirate ship. Edward and I joined Margareta and Bessie and the rest of the children as we pushed and shoved the heavy balls over the edge. We had barely started when Fred appeared in the middle of things. He had finally climbed down from the crow's nest and had come to join in the fun.

Each time a ball was balanced on the rail, the German children counted: "*Ein, zwei, drei, LOS,*" while we shouted, "One, two three, GO!" This was followed by a huge splash as the metal balls meant for destruction disappeared into their watery graves.

When the last cannonball had disappeared, the children prepared to climb back across the railing to the *Sunny Sloop* when Captain Lott stopped them. "Children," he said, "I would like for you to witness our next act. We are going to remove the pirate's flag from the flagpole. No more will it send a message of terror and destruction."

He moved to the center of the ship where the flagpole stood. Each child got a turn at pulling the cable that lowered the flag. When it had been removed from the rigging, he passed it around for all to see. Then he said, "We will leave the English flag a'furl, hoping that these people will return to their homeland in a peaceable manner."

It was midday by now. The sun rode high in the sky. I thought everything was ready for us to cut the ropes that still bound the two ships together when a movement on our ship caught my attention. Someone else was being led to climb over the railing to the other ship with their hands tied behind their backs. Why, it was our two stowaways, along with a girl wearing a red scarf on her head and a man with a similar scarf tied around his neck. Captain Lott, who was actually still parading around in his jacket and nightshirt without his trousers, addressed them, saying, "I hope you'll be able to get a fresh start when you reach England's shores. May you never forget your experiences on board the *Sunny Sloop*."

What a relief I felt to know that the stowaways and prisoners from our ship were being sent away to a new land and, hopefully, a new life.

After watching the removal of our prisoners, I returned to my vantage point on the main platform of the *Sunny Sloop*. I watched while our sailors lowered all the sails on the pirate ship. They climbed back across onto our ship where they unfurled all our sails. It looked as though we were about ready to cut loose from the pirate ship and be on our way.

Just before that happened, a movement on the *Fortune Seeker* caught my attention. Why, it was our little Fred—still on board the other ship. I started to holler at him, but realized he was talking to someone. Quickly, I climbed back over the rail and hurried toward him, curious to know what was going on.

When I got a little closer I realized he was standing in front of the captain of the pirate ship, who, like the others, was sitting on the floor, bound with ropes. I stopped a short distance away from them, but close enough to hear what Fred was saying. The man had an ugly scowl on his face. He turned his head so that he faced away from Fred, not meeting his eyes.

"Mr. Pirate, I was just wondering" Fred said, speaking in English, "when you was a little boy like me, did your Mama want you to grow up to be a mean old pirate? I don't think my Mama would want me to go around hurting people and taking their things, even when I'm grown up like you."

The captain attempted to ignore the child in front of him. He rolled his eyes upward and spat on the deck, but that didn't stop our Fred. He continued, "Since you don't have your gun and sword and stuff anymore, why don't you go back home and get a different job? Why don't you just quit being mean?"

I could tell by the activity back on the *Sunny Sloop* that they were making ready to cut loose from the pirate ship. I knew I needed to hurry and get my little brother back on board our own ship before we were left behind.

I moved closer to where he stood. "It's time to go now, Frederick," I called softly in English.

To my surprise, the pirate captain jerked his head around and looked right at me. It was then that I saw he was a very handsome man. He had a beard, but it was neatly shaped and clean, not like most of the other pirates. There was an earring in one ear. He wore a white shirt that opened halfway down his chest. It was tucked into his breeches. His boots, too, were clean and shiny. But the best feature about him was his eyes. They were the clearest, bluest eyes I had ever seen.

"What did you call him?" he asked me sharply,

"Frederick. That's his Christian name. Why?"

"Frederick," he said softly. "That be my name, too." He sat staring at Fred for a long moment, then said softly, "It be a long time since anybody called me that."

When Fred heard that, he grinned broadly. He looked down at the wooden cross that hung around his neck. "Since we both have the same name, I want to give you something." He took the cross from around his own neck and placed it over the captain's head where it nestled on his hairy chest. The leader of the pirates looked down at the cross, then back up at Fred. The two of them gazed at each other without saying a word.

Finally, in a husky voice, the pirate said, "Young Frederick, since you gave me a gift, I will give you one in return. Reach here in me shirt pocket. There be a gold coin which I have called me good luck piece for many a year. I think it worked today, because it let me meet you. Reach in and get it. I want ye to take it with ye to America. And good luck to ye, me boy."

Frederick did as he was told. He dug down into the pirate's shirt pocket and pulled the gold coin out. His snaggle-toothed grin stretched from ear to ear as he held the shiny gold piece in his hand. Instinctively, he leaned over and planted a kiss on the cheek of the pirate.

Just then we heard a cry. "Emma Mae! Fred!" It was John, leaping over the rail as he yelled to us.

Edward was right behind him. "Come on! The ship's ready to go! What are you doin' over here, anyway?"

"We're just talking to Mr. Frederick," Fred called out to them.

"Who?"

"Mr. Frederick," Fred answered simply. "I think he's going home to see about changing jobs."

I glanced at the pirate when he said that, just in time to catch a fleeting, one-sided smile.

Edward and John stopped behind us. From the looks on their faces, it was hard for them to believe that it was the captain of the pirate ship that Fred was referring to.

"That's good, Freddie, but we've got to go. Now!" Edward exclaimed.

"Just a minute," Captain Frederick called out in German as we started to move away. We stopped and looked back. The captain of the pirate ship, who a short time earlier had been threatening to steal the possessions and spill the blood of innocent travelers, gazed down at the cross that hung around his neck. He looked from the cross to young Fred, clutching his gold coin, and then to John. Still speaking in German, he asked, "Are these children in yer family?" His blue eyes were actually filled with tears.

John, too, looked misty eyed. He answered softly, "Yes. I'm happy to claim them as my family."

"You're a lucky man," the captain replied in a husky voice. "Cherish them."

Just then, Johann, standing next to the rails of the ships, interrupted this exchange as he shouted, "John! Children! Come now! They're ready to cut us loose!"

"We must go," John said urgently, gesturing to the three of us.

"Thanks for my coin, Mr. Frederick," Fred said as he turned to leave. "I'll never forget you."

As we backed away and I reached to take Fred's hand, I couldn't resist. I leaned over and kissed the pirate captain on the forehead. Then the four of us sprinted across the deck of the *Fortune Seeker*, jumped over the rail, and waved goodbye, just as the last rope that lashed the two ships together was cut.

As soon as that remaining tie was severed, the *Sunny Sloop*, her sails completely filled with the brisk September breeze, took off like an arrow. We gratefully made our way to our space near the lifeboats where we collapsed on our blankets.

"Do you think the pirate ship will come after us?" Edward asked John.

He replied, "*Nein*. We're sure the young pirate who was left untied will soon untie all his shipmates as well as our prisoners, and they will raise their sails again. But without weapons or cannons, it's not likely they will give chase to our shipload of travelers. Or to any others, for that matter."

The Graveyard

And so it was that, after the unexpected delay, the *Sunny Sloop* skimmed across the water again, headed for the promised land of America. We were safe! We were free! We were ready to celebrate!

A short time later, we were given the opportunity to do just that—celebrate. First we heard lively music coming from the quarterdeck. People streamed in from all parts of the ship. Captain Lott, who had finally had a chance to get to his quarters and get properly dressed, stood on the platform. He stuck his hand just inside the front of his jacket. His black boots gleamed in the late afternoon sun as he strutted back and forth.

When we were assembled, he began his speech. "*Danke, danke, danke,*" he called out. "What could have turned into a terrible tragedy became what just might possibly be the most peaceable attack by pirates ever experienced on the high seas. Your willingness to work together, your brave acts of courage, your spirit of cooperation and trust were wonderful to behold. I applaud you, every man, woman, and child, as well as my brave crew." He raised his hands above his head, clapping.

"Now I want you to applaud each other." Loud cheers and clapping came from all around the deck. Smiles and pats on the back were exchanged.

The captain raised his hand for silence and spoke again. "The *Sunny Sloop* is on a steady course, so with smooth sailing, we should arrive at the Port of New Orleans on schedule." This was followed by another burst of applause from people around the ship.

The captain called for attention one more time. "There was something else I was going to say . . . now what was it? Oh, yes. As for the three children who helped with the early morning warning and the translations, I want it to be known that they were godsends to the *Sunny Sloop* this day. Regardless of their status here, we are most grateful that they are along with us on this trip. And that's that."

With that remark, Captain Lott looked at the three of us standing nearby and, once again, began clapping his hands. The applause quickly spread to others around him. Out of the corner of my eye, I saw Tater and George standing on the outskirts of the crowd. At first they both seemed to be frowning at us, as usual; but, surprise of surprises, as the applause spread across the ship, both of them began to clap, too. Then—I could hardly believe my eyes—they both clapped with enthusiasm. I turned my head so I could look directly at Tater. Our eyes met, but there was no longer a glare in them. Instead, there was a smile that spread from his eyes to his lips.

When the short meeting ended, our entire family crowded into our space on deck. We laughed a lot as we compared stories and feelings we had experienced during the short-lived battle.

Tater showed up, too, but this time he sat near the back of the group, listening, laughing, and joining in with the exchanges. Not once did he refer to us as being stowaways or illegal passengers.

For supper that night we were in for a big surprise. Although the captain had told our sailors not to take food or supplies from the pirates' ship, he had apparently made one exception. Since our cooks were running short on fruit, we hadn't been served any for several days. But that night we had fried dried-apple pies. "Compliments of our friends, the English pirates from the *Fortune Seeker*," Captain Lott announced with a smile as he strutted about.

Before we went to sleep for the night, John came back around. It was quiet on the ship as people were settling in for an early bedtime. He didn't say a word—just sat there in the middle of our group of three.

For some reason, none of us said anything either. The unspoken communication was very strong. After a bit of time had passed, he stood and gave each of us a kiss on the top of our heads, simply whispering, "*Gute Nacht, my Kinderlein. Sei guter Hoffnung.*" Then he rose and walked away into the darkness.

CHAPTER 25

For the second morning in a row I awoke with a start. This time it was because of Fred's high-pitched voice.

"Look! Look!" he called out with excitement. "The sky is on fire! The water, too! Look, Emma Mae! Look, Edward! It's on fire! I know it is!"

As we rubbed the sleep from our eyes, we peered toward the east in the direction of the blazing light. It did, indeed, look as though that whole part of the world was on fire. The fiery red and orange of the clouds, streaked with golden yellow rays, spread for miles, lighting the entire eastern horizon. The reflection in the water was so bright, it was almost blinding. All around us, people were waking each other to see the spectacular sunrise.

"Wow, Freddie! That is really something, isn't it?" I said. "I'm glad you woke me up to see it." I placed my hands on his shoulders as we stood at the ship's rail. The ship was gliding smoothly across the water. The breeze felt fresh and clean.

Edward, who often was not inclined to wake up quickly, just looked at the sunrise for a minute and mumbled, "Red at morning, sailors' warning."

I jerked my head around to look at him, but he had already left to go back to sleep. His remark, though, gave me an uneasy feeling.

Now that I was awake, I decided to get the journal out of my pocket and write about the pirate episode from the day before. In my usual, enthusiastic way, I thought I would also write a description of the blood-red sunrise. I flipped the page, only to find it was the last page in the tablet. Why, there was no room left to write about another experience. I could almost envision the words "The End" written there. That, too, gave me an unsettled feeling.

The rest of the morning passed in a normal way, with visits from our family being the main agenda. Fred was training Clyde to do more tricks, which kept us entertained. Even John's youngest sisters, Katarina and Nellie, had begun to accept the little gray rat as a pet.

After a while, our family, except for John, left to go below. Everything seemed to be going along as usual, but with two exceptions. One, the quiet, serious look on John's face, and, two, the choppiness of the sea that had grown as the day wore on.

It wasn't until mid-afternoon that thunder began to rumble off in the distance. Edward and I felt drawn to the ship's rail, looking at the gathering storm. Fred, sensing our uneasiness, came and stood between us. Not a word was spoken.

Then we were aware of a fourth person standing in the group huddled at the rail. It was John. He stood behind Fred and put an arm around the shoulders of both Edward and me. We looked up at him, but none of us felt compelled to say anything for many long minutes.

After watching the approaching storm for a bit and feeling the rise and fall of the ship on the water, I heard movement behind us. I turned around to see our great-grandparents, Johann and Mary Katherine, along with the four girls. We all sat down together by the lifeboats.

Edward, Fred, and I looked at each other. Instinctively, we knew that our time with our family was about to end. Looking at my great-grandmother, I broke the silence by saying, "I know this whole experience has been like a fairy tale that even the queen of storytelling wouldn't believe." She nodded, with tears in her eyes.

I continued, "I wouldn't believe it myself, except I know it has truly happened."

The waves were getting higher. Up, up, up, then a pause before going down, down, down on the other side. The lightning and thunder were moving closer as we continued to sit there, absorbing each other's company.

Mary Katherine said, "What a blessing you have been to all of us during these past few weeks. However it was that you were brought to us, it would be selfish of us not to wish you a safe return to your family."

"We have a picture of you two hangin' on our wall back home," Edward said, gesturing to our great-grandparents. "That's how we recognized you not long after we got here."

I added, "We'll think of you often when we return—every time we look at your picture."

In spite of the growing threat of the storm, another person joined us on deck. It was none other than Tater. Fred, who was sitting in John's lap and holding his pet in his hands, looked at Tater and said, "There's a boy at our school who looks just like you. He's the one that got us in trouble at school one day. But in a way, he kind of helped us be able to come here and meet all of you."

The lightning flashed closer now. The booming of the thunder was all around us. The rest of the people, except for the deckhands who were managing the sails, had gone inside long before. Still we huddled on the quilts by the lifeboats.

The storm was just about upon us now. As the first raindrops began to fall, Johann and Mary Katherine reached out their arms to hold us close.

"I don't want to leave yet," cried Fred, just before another flash of lightning.

"Here, my little Fred, I have made you a new cross," John called out. "You can take it with you along with some wonderful memories of crossing the Atlantic with your ancestors. As much as I hate to see our time together end, I think it's time for you to go."

Johann and Mary Katherine nodded their heads. The four girls smiled through their tears. Johann spoke loudly, above the sounds of the stormy sea, "I have a request to make of you, my children. It's hard for me to believe you can't speak the German language in real life. Is that true? You can't speak German?"

"*Nein!*" we all three responded in unison.

"Then learn it!" he yelled back. "It's part of your heritage." He bobbed his head up and down, smiling broadly.

"*Ja!* We will! We will!" the three of us answered together.

"This has been the most unusual experience I've ever had in my life." Johann said." He was really yelling now, in order to be heard above the noise of the storm. "It's impossible to understand, but how happy it makes me to know that children such as you are some of our own descendants."

Mary Katherine, in her usual gentle manner, called out, "When a good thing ends, don't feel sad; for memories can last forever."

The three of us burst into laughter. "That's exactly what our Papa always says. 'When a good thing ends, don't feel sad; for memories can last forever.'" When I said that, the glum looks on the faces of our family all turned to smiles.

The storm was really getting wild. Waves crashed onto the deck, swirling around our feet. A bright bolt of lightning split the air, followed immediately by a crash of thunder. Still we hung on to each other.

John shouted. "I'm sure there's a connection between your coming here in a thunderstorm and going back in a thunderstorm. Don't you think so?"

Edward, Fred, and I looked at one another as a thunderclap shook the ship.

"We think so, too," I hollered, nodding my head. The pounding of the waves and the sounds of the wind and storm were tremendous.

He yelled again. "Since you told us you said the words 'Sunny Sloop' to get here, then the three of you need to stand in a group, holding hands, and say 'Sunny Slope' just as there is a flash of lightning. Maybe it will have the reverse effect, and you'll find yourselves back in Kentucky."

"It's worth a try," Edward yelled, starting to get up.

"All right now," John hollered. "Get out there and say your magic words, you three. And good luck to you all! Be of good cheer! I love you! *Auf wiedersehen!*"

"We love you, Grandpapa! We love all the rest of you, too! *Auf wiedersehen!*"

The three of us ran to the middle of the deck just as the ship was mounting a wave. We looked back to see the little group huddled in the downpour of rain, waving and blowing kisses.

Up, up, up! We grabbed hands in a little circle as the ship paused at the crest of the wave. Then, just before it started down, there was a tremendous flash of lightning. We yelled "Sunny Slope," all at the same time.

And we never went down on the other side of the wave!

CHAPTER 26

The next thing we knew, the ground under our feet was steady. The rain still pounded us and the wind kept howling. There was a loud crash of thunder, but we never came down off that wave. The reason? We were standing near the graveyard in the middle of the Singleton Field.

John's idea had worked. We were home!

"Emma Mae? Edward? Fred? Where in the world have you been? It's getting late!"

It was Clarence, calling to us from the side of the road.

"I can't believe it! We're really back! We're safe!"

We all three jumped up and down in the middle of the field in the pouring down rain, holding hands and laughing.

"Come on, simpletons! Don't you have enough sense to come in out of the rain? Mama's got supper ready! She sent me to find you."

"Why, Clarence hasn't changed a bit!" I said with a smile. "And it sounds like it's still the same day we left."

We started to run toward home, but suddenly I stopped. When I stopped, so did the two boys. I turned and looked toward the cemetery plot at the end of the field. While the rain pelted down, drenching our hair and clothes, I felt compelled to stare at the gravestones, now looking plain, gray, and wet in the distance. Edward and Fred both stood silently at my side. Thunder rumbled.

"Are you people nuts?" called Clarence from the road. "You can stand there 'til you drown, if you want to. I'm going to the house." And with that he took off at a run.

It was precisely at that moment that the strangest thing happened! I suddenly had an overwhelming feeling that maybe we hadn't been gone at all! When I said this to my brothers, they said they had the same feeling.

"But it did happen," I said emphatically. "I know it did. The question is, are we going to tell anybody about it?"

"Do you think they would believe us?" Edward responded. He scratched above his left ear the way he always does when he's not sure about something.

"I know *I* wouldn't believe us," Fred added.

"Why don't we just keep our secret to ourselves, then?" I asked. "We each have our own special things to help us remember."

"I won't need any help. I'll always . . . just remember." Edward whispered those last words with feeling.

With the rain soaking us to the skin, we started walking toward the barbed wire fence at the edge of the Singleton Field when I stopped again. There was a distant rumble of thunder.

"All right," I said. "Since we all agree not to share our secret, you'd better give me your keepsakes so I can tuck them away for now. At least we have these things to help us keep it in mind." Edward handed me his carved ship while Fred pulled his cross and the pirate's gold coin out of his pocket. I put them in the large pocket of my dress, along with my own journal.

Suddenly Fred said, "Uh-oh, Emma Mae. You have one more thing you need to hide."

"What do you mean, Freddie," I asked, looking down at his rain-splattered face.

"This!" he answered, pulling something from the other pocket of his pants. It was small and gray. Its bright little eyes looked up at us from between Fred's cupped hands.

"What in the world . . ." I began. Then we all started laughing, standing there in the middle of the thunderstorm.

"Fred, you brought Clyde with you!" shouted Edward. "Talk about a keepsake!"

I smiled at my brothers. "I think you'd better take care of this secret on your own, little Fred. I'm afraid I'd scream every time it wiggled in my pocket." Fred grinned his snaggle-toothed grin as he stuck the baby rat back into his own pocket. "And you'll have to keep it hidden until you can act like you've tamed one of our own rats from the corn crib," I added.

The steady ground felt strange to my legs after having been on board the ship for so long, but I knew it was time for us to go home. Another sizzling streak of lightning flashed, followed by a clap of thunder. "We need to get going. Come on, boys! Beat you to the house!"

And with that, we sprinted across the field, through the fence, down the road, and over the railroad tracks as we raced toward home. We went dripping into the house, and there was our dear Mama, waiting to dry us off with soft dry towels. "I'm sure glad you got home safely," she said. "That's a terrible storm out there with enough wind to blow you all the way across the ocean."

We looked at each other and smiled. It was good to be home again. Then I looked at the portrait on the wall. It was the same picture of our great-grandparents, Johann and Mary Katherine, from Bavaria, Germany, which I had seen so many times. But, can you believe it? This time they smiled at me. And, I promise you, I think they winked!

CHAPTER 27

The next day Edward and I did our after-school chores early before slipping away to the graveyard in the Singleton Field. The sun was sinking down like a giant orange ball over the tops of the trees. Strange-looking shafts of light streaked down onto the gravestones. Once again it gave off an eerie, uncanny feeling. Birds twittered in the nearby woods and insects buzzed.

"I'm as nervous as a cat," I whispered, "but I think we need to do this."

I went straight to my great-grandparents' gravestone. I had picked a small bouquet of late-summer marigolds from Mama's garden and put them in a pint fruit jar filled with water. I knelt down by the monument, putting the jar of flowers there. Then I sat down and leaned my head back against the large stone, just as I had done before. As I twisted the tiny gold chain around my neck, a strange quietness settled over the place. And over me.

I looked at Edward on the other side of the cemetery. He had constructed a small cross out of some narrow boards he had found in Papa's woodshed. Except for the tap-tap-tapping sound as he drove the cross into the ground in front of our grandparents' tombstone, there was silence.

Edward sat down beside their grave and looked across at me. The setting sun had begun its spectacular evening show in the western sky. The orange streaks of light grew brighter. As the sunbeams touched the tombstones, the entire graveyard started to glow. Then, in the quietness of the place, it began again.

The scene seemed to get wavy and distorted. The beams and shadows from the sun became flickering flashes of light. Edward and I looked at each other across the space, waiting for the strange sounds that we felt sure would rise from the ground between us. But this time there were no sounds. Just a feeling of quietness . . . and peace.

Gradually the flashes began to fade. We sat there absorbing the silence until the sun's rays dimmed and the flashing stopped.

"We owe our ancestors a lot, don't we, Ed?" I asked softly.

"Yes, we do. And aren't we glad we found out so much about them in such an excitin' way?"

"I expect we'll be the best prepared students in school to give our reports next week. I guess we have to give Miss Stone some of the credit for what happened, though, since she was the one who got us thinking about our ancestors."

Edward nodded.

After another pause, I said, "You know what? Even as exciting as our adventure was, I'll have to admit, it's good to be home and getting back to normal. School was actually fun today. Even Miss Stone was nice."

"I agree," Edward said, still speaking across the distance between the graves. He stood up and walked toward me. "By the way, did you see me talkin' to Big Bad Clyde and his brother after school?"

"Yes, I did. What was that all about?"

Edward sat down beside me. The small creek that ran beside the graveyard trickled peacefully. "I asked them what had been goin' on in the woods next to the cemetery when I saw them that day, and they just laughed.

"Clyde explained that the neighborhood boys were having their secret meeting, like they do every week. They had met that afternoon and were cuttin' up just for the fun of it when I saw them. The reason they had a gun is because they were gettin' ready to have target practice."

"Wait a minute! Are you telling me that our neighborhood boys actually have a secret group?" I asked Edward.

He nodded. "Yep. Clyde told me all about it. He said they're just a group of fellows who like to help people in our neighborhood when they need it. They've been growin' vegetables in that meadow in the middle of the woods all summer so they can share them with that family who moved here with a lot of little children. When they have work days, Clyde puts his old hat on the fencepost by the road so the others'll know it's a work day.'"

"I can hardly believe it. How can anybody who acts as mean as Clyde be doing such a kind thing? That's quite a shock to me," I said.

"It was to me, too. But do you want to know another surprise?"

"Sure. Tell me."

"Clarence is in their group."

"What?" I looked at Edward with big eyes. "Our brother is in the secret group?"

Edward nodded as he continued his story. "I couldn't believe it, either. I just smiled and shook my head when he told me."

"What else did he say?"

"The two of us apologized about the fight and shook hands. When Clyde walked away, his brother Toby stayed behind to explain. He said Clyde likes to put on an act to scare people so they won't know he really is a nice person."

"Well, he sure had *me* fooled," I said.

"Me, too. And everybody else we know."

Edward scratched above his left ear with a thoughtful look on his face. "You know, I think I'll mention all this to Clarence. I might like to be part of the group next summer."

"That's a good idea, Ed, even though I'm still having trouble thinking of Clyde as having a good side."

Edward laughed. Then we both sat in silence, absorbing the stillness and the sudden near-darkness that follows a brilliant sunset. A crescent moon began to glow in the west.

I interrupted the quietness, sighing as I stood to leave. "I almost hate to leave this special place where we first started getting acquainted with our ancestors."

"Yeah," Edward agreed, "and the friends of our ancestors, like Tater, who came to North America at the same time. Who would ever have thought that Tater would be Clyde's granddaddy?"

As we walked across the Singleton Field toward home, suddenly there was one more flare of golden light from the sun. It seemed to bounce off our grandparents' gravestone. A soft voice floated from somewhere far away.

"You fooo-u-n-d-d me. You fooo-u-n-d-d me. Be of good cheer. *Auf Wiedersehen.*"

Tears sprang to my eyes. "That is so like our grandfather," I whispered. "Aren't we glad we got to spend some time with him and the others?"

"I'll never forget them as long as I live," responded Edward.

We held hands as we walked quietly from the graveyard, which now seemed more sacred than ever before.

That night when Mama tucked me in bed I said, "Clarence told me today that you and Papa have decided to let him go back to school for another year."

"Yes," she said. "After our discussion on the porch the other night before school started, we thought it over again and decided we could get by without his help for one more year. Clarence was tickled to death when we told him." She smiled.

"I'm glad, Mama. There are so many things in this family that make me glad." I sighed. "Like, I'm really happy that you and Papa are going to let Edward and me take German lessons."

"You don't know how pleased we were when you asked about that. We've always wanted to know more of the language ourselves, so you might just teach all of us what you learn."

"That would be wonderful, Mama. We can have family lessons."

Mama nodded her head and kissed me. She reached over and stroked my cat that lay at the foot of the bed. "I hope you and Maggie both get a good night's sleep. *Gute Nacht*, my little *Fraulein*."

"*Gute Nacht, Mutter*."

As Mama walked away with the coal oil lamp, I held my doll Maizey close. Darkness filled the space around me; my eyelids closed. I was almost asleep, to dream of sailing ships and pirates and remarkable people to love when an idea popped into my head. My eyes popped open! I sat straight up in bed!

If this unbelievable adventure happened on board a ship, I thought, I wonder . . . could something else magical happen at another time and in another place? Hmmm.

I lay back down and, twirling my gold necklace around my finger, closed my eyes, this time drifting off to sleep . . . with a smile on my face.

THE END?

AUTHOR'S NOTE

Many of the stories in this book reflect what I was told during my childhood days about how my ancestors crossed the ocean to start a new life in America in 1845. My family's stories are similar to the tales of countless Americans whose families also came to this country during the 19th century.

Since I wanted to preserve some of the anecdotes, I have incorporated them into a fast-moving tale of a fantastical journey that takes my protagonists back in time where they join their ancestors in the voyage across the Atlantic Ocean toward North America. I have taken some stories and facts and entwined them into a story of fantasy and adventure, especially to be enjoyed by children . . . and readers of any age!

CPSIA information can be obtained at www.ICGtesting.com
Printed in the USA
LVOW080335241112

308422LV00004B/10/P